FIREREND

Published by *of the page press*

Copyright © 2025 by Emma Kennedy

ISBN 979-8-9913258-0-6

Cover art by Charles Utting

Interior art by Emma Kennedy

To my city—Los Angeles.

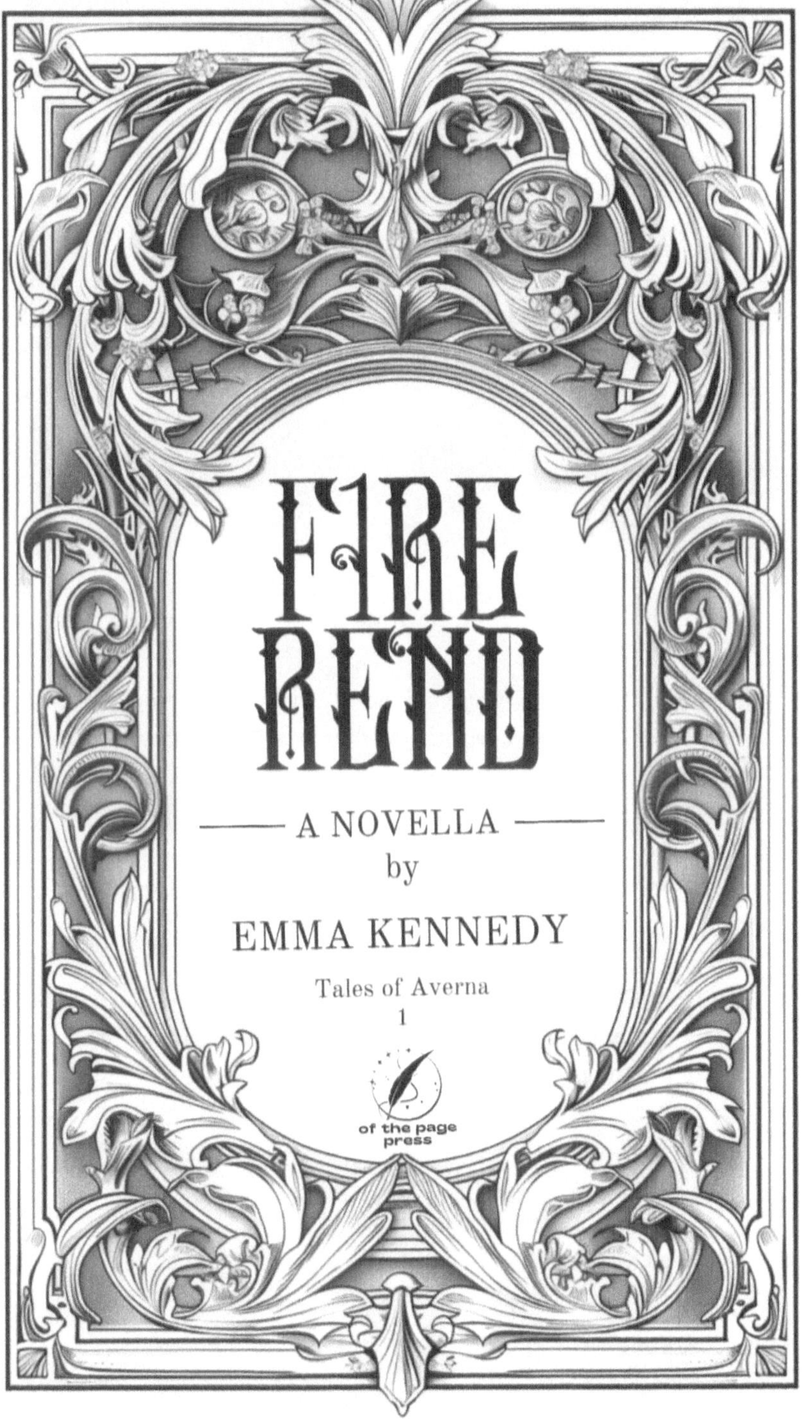

FIRE REND
A NOVELLA
by
EMMA KENNEDY
Tales of Averna
1
of the page
press

GLOSSARY & PRONUNCIATIONS

<u>**PEOPLE**</u>

<u>**THE FOOLS:**</u> *The newest guild in the underworld. They quickly rose to notoriety but have recently fallen on hard times, teetering on the edge of disbanding.*

Nymm (NIM)

The brains. Civarran. She excels in the shadows. Her leadership is unquestioned, although it was not always so.

Auren (OAR-en)

The blade. He trains and evaluates all new recruits. He is second in command to Nymm, despite joining two years prior to her.

Ilia (ill-EE-uh)

The keeper. After being injured in a robbery gone wrong, she joined the Guild. Ilia cooks for all members and takes care of household duties.

Tulvar (TOLL-var)

The alchemist. They create all manner of potions, poultices, and solutions for the Guild's needs.

Virgil (VER-jull)

The enforcer. Problems within and outside of the Guild are handled at Virgil's discretion—which usually means his fists.

Téo (Thay-oh)

The recruiter. In charge of securing new members and earning contracts for the Guild.

Ivan (EYE-van)

The lackey. A newer member of the guild, he's still proving himself.

Milo (MY-lo)

The newest recruit, close in age to Ivan and just as eager.

THE UNDERWORLD: *Any guild that works outside the bounds of the law is part of the underworld. They operate by their own code and will do whatever is asked of them, for the right amount of gold.*

Shae (shay)

Civarran. Works at the Gilded Abyss and is in the Fixer Guild. The Fixers facilitate contracts for all of the other guilds.

THE CAPITAL: *Oberon is the largest city in the island country of Averna. It is also home to the Emissary, ruler of Averna, and has felt the strongest effects of the Valmaris occupation.*

Allara (uh-LAR-uh)

Has no trade, but makes do with odd jobs and her wits. Sole caretaker of her sister, Daia.

Daia (DAY-uh)

Allara's older sister. Fell ill eight years prior and remains in bed. Requires weekly medications.

Taran (TARE-en)

Fisherman by trade, troublemaker by heart. Fourth-born to the Casilars, and Allara's closest friend.

Roan (RO-en)

Successful poet, rose from the Outer Circle to the Middle Circle. They often supply Allara and other Outer Circle residents with means of earning gold.

Cyrie (SEAR-ee)

Auren's sister, brilliant with numbers and studying to be a physician.

LOCATIONS

AVERNA

Averna is an island country well-known for its agreeable climate, fertile farmland, and high population of mages. Occupied by Valmaris in 1456, Averna still flourishes with exports like olives, figs, and grain. Pre-conquering, Averna was independent, with a polytheistic religion and a strong connection to magic. It was considered a world power. Post-conquering, magic has faded out with the generations, and public worship of the gods is becoming more dangerous by the day.

<u>OBERON</u>

Oberon is the capital of the island country of Averna. Being the northernmost city, it contains the busiest ports and is considered the center of trade. The Emissary's Hold makes up the center of Oberon, commonly referred to as the Inner Circle. Surrounding are the capital's nobles, artists, and other influential citizens. While still incredibly wealthy, they informally make up the Middle Circle. Eighty percent of Oberon's population live in what is deemed the Outer Circle, a dense, cramped place.

<u>CIVARA</u>

Civara was a city to the southwest of Oberon, surrounded by mountains and farther inland. It was originally a settlement of natural-born mages, who populated the area due to the large concentration of crystal mines. They established the College of Enchantments and became one of the world's leaders in magic and education of mages. In one of the most decisive battles of Valmaris's[RF1] conquering of Averna, Civara was destroyed. Most of its inhabitants were killed by invading soldiers, while the rest were indentured to Valmaris to serve as court mages or laborers. Magic was then outlawed unless performed in an official capacity.

<u>VALMARIS</u>

First established in 302, it is the largest country on the continent, with an expansive navy and land infantry. Famed for combat, they've launched several successful conquests of neighboring civilizations. When they expanded to Averna, they signed a treaty that allowed Averna to retain their own government and leadership structure, provided that they cede to Valmaris's will. They breed a hardy, strong people, but have no natural-born mages.

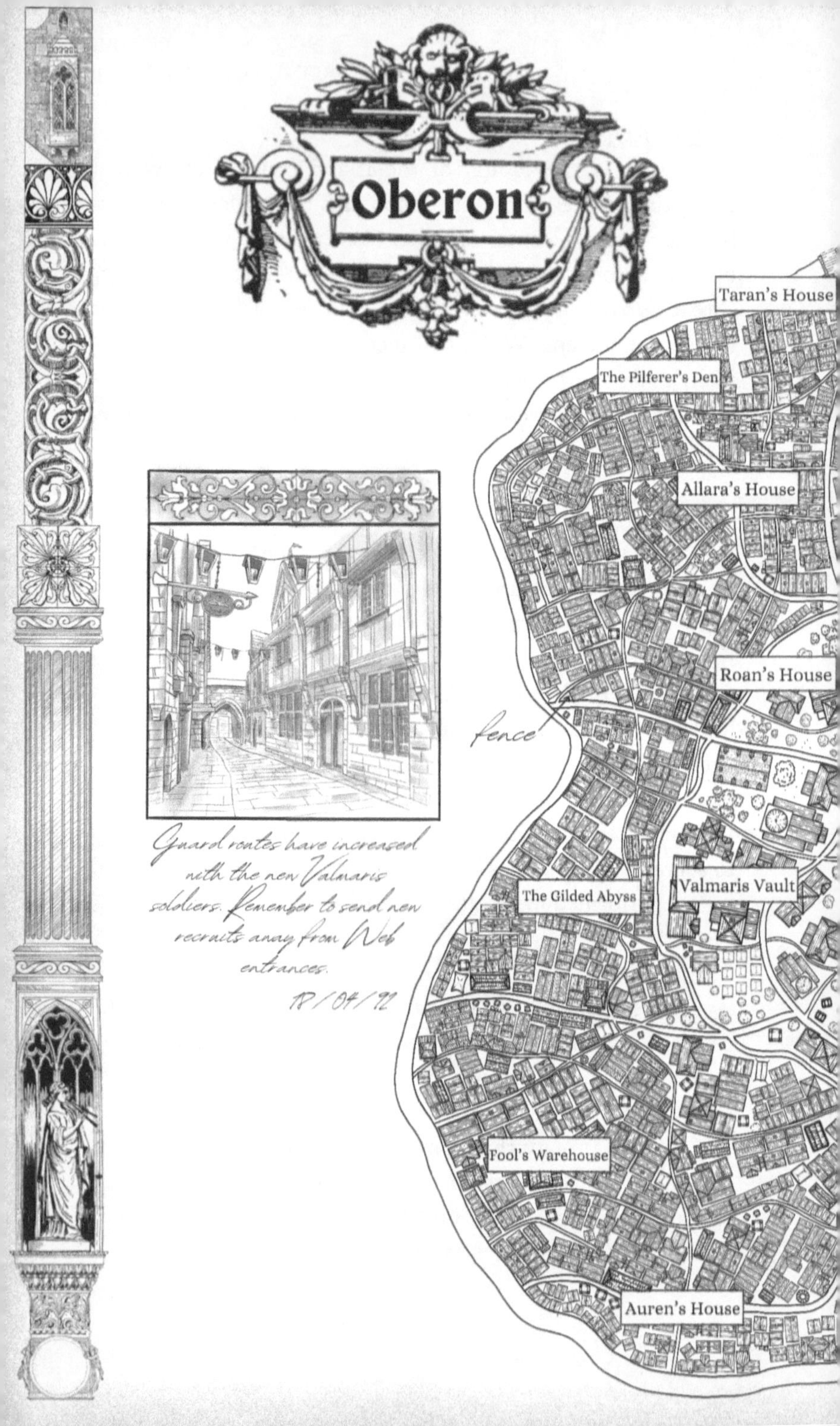

Oberon
Guard routes have increased with the new Valmaris soldiers. Remember to send new recruits away from Web entrances.
TP / 04 / 92
fence
Taran's House
The Pilferer's Den
Allara's House
Roan's House
The Gilded Abyss
Valmaris Vault
Fool's Warehouse
Auren's House

Property of Nymm
Give me my books back
- Auren
The Docks
The Flying Fish
fence
out of business
The Bookseller
N
W   E
S
The Keep
The Web Entrance
Festival Courtyard
Guard Tower
shift change at
3rd & 8th bell
last
The Capital of Averna
1490 AC

AUTHOR'S NOTE

This information contains spoilers, but if you feel you need to be prepared prior, I highly encourage you to check the content information below.

This book contains the following content that may be upsetting to some readers:

THE FOLLOWING INFORMATION CONTAINS SPOILERS
BLOOD
CLASSISM
COLONIALISM
CONFINEMENT
DEATH
FIRE/FIRE INJURY
GENOCIDE
KIDNAPPING
VIOLENCE

Moths to a Flame

CHAPTER ONE
ALLARA

Like almost every day in the capital, it was annoyingly sunny. Allara tapped her fingers on the counter as she waited for the bookkeeper to return, glancing out the small window to her left as people walked by. She could hear laughter, arguments, and the faintest melody of the bard at the tavern down the road. Sighing, she picked at a fleck of dirt under her nails. *Gods, this is taking forever.*

When the bookkeeper finally returned, Allara had cleaned under each nail twice over. He cleared his throat. "These are some … odd requests you have, Miss Allara."

"They're not for me," she replied, trying to keep the frustration out of her voice. Mr. Fonte was a kind man. He'd given her sister, Daia, sheet music for free for almost ten years. But it wasn't Allara's fault that her client desired ridiculously obscure books. She had assumed when she took this job that it would be quick, and that she could be back out on another job by evening. Yet here she was, wasting away the late midday in a dusty bookshop. It seemed that her client, Roan, had an uncommon taste in literature. Two of the five books she was tasked with retrieving for them were causing quite some trouble. She was inclined to feel bad for Mr. Fonte, who usually knew his way around the shop as if he could navigate it blind. But every ring of the bells while she wasn't working meant more time she wasn't getting paid.

"Give me a day or two. I'm not sure I have the books you need; you might have to try a more specialized store," the bookkeeper said as he slid his wire-frame glasses farther up the bridge of his nose.

"I'm supposed to get this done today, sir," Allara replied.

"Who are the books for?"

"Roan, Mr. Fonte."

His sigh was long-suffering. "Oh, I shouldn't have bothered to ask. It's just like them to be after such an … eclectic assortment. Alright…" Mr. Fonte straightened his glasses. "Come back in an hour or so, and I'll see what I can do."

"Thank you, sir! I appreciate it!" Allara beamed as she backed toward the door before he could change his mind. She flew out, hearing the satisfying chime of the bell as she regained her freedom. Since it was past the midday meal, she decided to head to a tavern and see about getting any leftover food from the rush. Most of the taverns in the area saved enough scraps that she could barter for. But the chef of the tavern in the wharf district, the Flying Fish, sometimes slipped her fresh rolls and ale for nothing in return. Allara hoped the gods had a decent meal in store for her.

The cobblestones under her feet weren't clean enough to reflect the sun, but she imagined the ones in the Inner Circle were gleaming with the soft beams. The buildings around her were painted in chipped coats of deep cerulean, marigold, and emerald, worn and rotting, despite the tithes the Outer Circle paid each season for maintenance—tithes that most likely were funneled into extravagant projects in the Inner or Middle Circles instead of theirs.

Shops displayed bright, eye-catching banners in anticipation of the upcoming summer festival. It was never too early to try to make a profit off the tourists that would flock to Oberon in the coming weeks.

As she rounded the corner to where the Flying Fish was, she saw patrons spilling outside to listen to Sana playing her lute, careful to stay on the tavern's front terrace or risk being fined for "unlawful gatherings." Sana was talented with most instruments, but that wasn't why she was one of the most popular bards in the area. She had long hair colored like honey and a smile as bright as the sun. She'd be just as popular if she couldn't hit a single note.

Allara brushed past the crowd to head inside as Sana caught her eye, giving her a quick wink, and Allara felt her cheeks redden. It seemed she wasn't immune to Sana's charm either. She caught the attention of Van, the head chef since before Allara had been born, and gave the most earnest look she could muster. Van rolled his eyes, but cracked a small grin, gesturing for Allara to find a table in the back.

It was between bells, and most of the patrons were finished eating and back to work. Only the riffraff like herself would be out and about at this hour with not much to do. Not that Allara ever had much to do with no consistent work or gold to spend.

She hadn't been beholden to the chimes of the bells since she was in school. They rang out several times a day to indicate when to eat, work, close shop, and go home. And in the past decade, the bells for prayer had slowly dwindled to nothing. Allara would never get used to the loss. Only those with special passes, legitimate or otherwise, could get away with staying out past the final bell, or risk jail time. Allara had always made it a habit to carry a counterfeit or two on her, just in case. She patted down the special sleeve in her satchel to make sure she still had a few. She had to remember after this job to—

"Hey, troublemaker."

Allara looked up and saw Taran, her closest friend, and one of the many suppliers of her odd jobs. Taran managed to *find* things while working full-time on his family's fishing boat, and he gave them to Allara to sell. It wasn't exactly within the law, but the sunken pirates and drunk merchants he robbed never complained.

At night, Taran often found less acceptable means of income. There had been a period last winter when he had taken up boxing. He would sneak to her house for powders and creams past dawn to cover his cuts and bruises. Allara was glad when that phase had passed, and she no longer had to pray to the gods for his safety each night.

"Hey, fish food," Allara replied with a smirk, and smacked his arm. "It's been weeks. I was hoping the sea had gotten you this time."

"Alas, maybe next time," Taran said with a dramatic eye roll. Allara would never admit that she was happy to see him as he squeezed his way onto the too-small bench next to her, clumsily elbowing her in the ribs. He smelled like the sea. Allara always wondered how he managed to smell like that rather than the barrels of fish he spent the day hauling.

Taran had been a scrawny kid all throughout their classes. But once he started helping out on his father's boat, loading and unloading pounds of supplies, he started to put some muscle on. His wavy auburn hair stuck to his temples and glistened in the glow of the tavern. It must have been a busy day. There was a sparkle of mischief in his amber eyes that both thrilled and terrified her. She knew what that look meant.

"Well, cut to the point, then," she prodded.

"I don't know what you're expecting me to say."

She gave him her best stare-down. They were both stubborn and strong-willed, and more often than not, she was the one to give in first.

When Taran only shrugged, Allara scoffed, bringing her hand to her heart. "Oh, please. I can tell you're preparing a whole speech."

At that, he laughed and shook his head, but the laughter sounded forced somehow. "We can't talk about it here."

"Seriously?"

"Yes," he replied, hushed. "Let's enjoy our meal, and then we'll go back to my house, and I'll explain everything to you."

She sighed. "I'm in the middle of a job, so we'll have to go to the Open Book first."

She was sure Taran was working up to some kind of clever remark before a server approached their table. Allara's stomach twisted in anticipation, and she recited a quick prayer. She had no coin to spare, but maybe the gods could be kinder to Van than they were to her.

They left the tavern arm in arm, satisfied from a shared plate of fish. Oberon was many things, but it definitely had delicious food. Being the port city closest to the continent, it had access to the best spices and ingredients. Allara couldn't imagine living somewhere where she didn't know the taste of saffron and carp, even if she'd only ever tasted the throwaway scraps. Maybe that made her more like the rest of the citizens in the capital than she cared to admit.

They walked back into the shop to find Mr. Fonte absent.

"What do you need a bunch of books for anyways, Allara? We all know you're not civilized enough to enjoy reading."

She stuck her tongue out at Taran. "The books are for Roan. They're giving me thirty gold to pick these up."

Taran gave a low whistle. She knew the pay was shit. If there was an easier way to make money, she wished she would have figured it out by now.

The jobs this season were much more infrequent than she had anticipated, and with Taran's long absences, she couldn't always rely on his pilfering. She wasn't much good at things like sewing or smithing or singing, as much as she had tried. It bothered the hell out of her. And she'd rather starve than work at one of the gambling halls. All she could do was scrape by on wits and sheer determination, and it wasn't enough.

"Is that you, Miss Allara?" Mr. Fonte called as he made his way back to the front counter. There were strands of his wiry hair sticking out at odd angles, and his glasses were smudged so badly that Allara could barely see his eyes behind them. She felt a twinge of guilt at the thought that while she and Taran were laughing and eating, he had been shuffling through stacks of books on his own.

"Well, it wasn't easy, but I've found your books."

Allara nodded. "Thank you, sir."

"Now, these aren't any kind of books I've come across before—don't know how long they've been back there. You tell Roan that they need to take very good care of these. Would you do that, please?"

"Yes, I will, sir. I appreciate the help. How much will it be?"

"Ten gold, miss," the bookkeeper replied as he polished his glasses with a small cloth.

"Have a good night, Mr. Fonte," Allara replied, sliding

fifteen gold onto the counter and dragging Taran along with her before the bookkeeper could protest.

Allara took a deep breath of the briny air. They had a long walk to Roan's house. She felt dead on her feet, wishing she could just be back in the glorified sack she called a bed. When she was younger, she would have only just been starting her nighttime adventures, but things just weren't like that for her anymore.

Taran tapped Allara on the nose. "What are you thinking about?"

"Planning what I'm going to spend my twenty gold on."

"Technically, it's only fifteen, because you overpaid for the books."

"Well, he went to such trouble..." Allara frowned and began shuffling through the contents of the books in the stack. Poetry... herbalism ... and then a black leather-bound book so odd that Allara almost faltered in her stride. It had bizarre sketches of hands, crystals—birds, even. And it wasn't in Avernan or Valmaran. Allara had never seen a language like it before. Her sense reacted to the pages, a feeling seeping into her hands, burning so hot that she fumbled not to drop it.

Wrong—it felt so wrong. Whatever Roan wanted it for, well, Allara paid it no more mind. She just needed her gold, and the rest didn't matter. She never wanted to sense something so awful ever again.

They walked along the uneven cobblestones. Allara was so sure of where each street and alleyway led, as if her muscles had remembered it for her. She had been to so many parts of the city for so many reasons that she had seen every secret and forgotten part of the capital. The closer to the Keep you went, the higher and more ornate the buildings got. There were some in the Inner Circle that had four or five stories. Allara couldn't imagine what a person would need all of that space for.

She glanced at Taran, still wearing his work clothes: a dark green tunic and gray pants, tucked into tall leather boots. She supposed the boots were to help keep his feet dry —not that it was very likely to be accomplished working in the middle of the sea.

Since they'd graduated from school nine summers prior, she'd seen him less and less. After his oldest brother, Elric, was robbed and killed, his father had had trouble earning enough out on the boat alone. And if they didn't meet the minimums set by the port guards, then they'd lose their spot at the docks. So, while Taran had been given a choice, there wasn't really any other option but to help his father and join his trade. It wasn't going to be Saylin, newly wed, or either of his younger brothers.

Allara sometimes wondered what he would have done if his father hadn't asked that of him. She didn't think he minded much; it probably bothered her more than it did him.

He'd been pretty popular in their class, because unlike her, he was friendly with everyone. It wasn't that Allara didn't try to be nice, but growing up, it seemed people always sensed an *otherness* to her. She had unexplained dreams and visions, and often knew things she had no business knowing. She'd thought to be helpful with the information she gleaned, but others always found it unnerving. She'd learned after a while to just hold her tongue.

Why Taran had gone to the effort to get to know her was beyond her, but she was grateful for it. He was one of the only real friends she had, and some selfish part of her was glad he had stayed in the capital too. This time of year was their favorite for earning extra gold, and she had started to worry she'd be on her own this year for the festival.

Every year, the priests held a prayer and festival in honor of Oberon's patron goddess, Thiane, goddess of light and the harvest. The festivities happened during the longest day of the year, when there were only two hours of moonlight. It was meant to thank Thiane for the climate she bestowed upon the island of Averna, which allowed fertile land for crops and smooth seas to trade goods on. For Allara, it just meant more pockets to pick and the wonders of watching the fire dancers perform. She'd heard rumors that the festival was going to be canceled, but she knew the Emissary would never let that stand. No matter that they were now a territory of Valmaris; they were still Averna, and subjugation could not erase their identity.

They wove their way through the curving and narrow streets, getting closer and closer to the Middle Circle's border. Shoulders brushed against one another as they navigated the dense brush of the crowds. Allara tucked her satchel neatly against her side, mindful that with the steady increase in tourists, there was also a steady increase in pickpockets. She knew their tricks; it was what she would do too.

They finally reached the checkpoint, and Allara held out her work pass that Roan had provided for the day. It was the only way to travel from the Outer Circle to the other two. Tourists had temporary passes, and tradespeople had work passes like Allara's and Taran's. Nobles never needed a pass. The only time the borders opened freely was during the festival each year. They were waved through after shuffling through one of the many lines. Allara hated the border, feeling as though she were a sheep in a flock rather than a person.

They finally arrived at the street Roan lived on, and Allara let out a sigh of relief. After an incredibly slow day, she was desperate for what meager payment she was owed, and hoped Roan was in a good mood. They ambled their way up to the house, a two-story and ridiculously over-decorated structure. It was made of brick and dark wood, with two columns framing the doorway. From the first level's balcony, there were bright purple flags embroidered in silver with a pen and a rose—Roan's own self-designed crest. Crests were typically for guilds and other such groups, but they were also for those with a very inflated sense of self.

They walked up the stairs and knocked on the front door. Allara could hear the very soft melody of a flute coming from inside. Growing impatient, she knocked louder. Taran gave her an amused look, and she just shrugged.

"JUST A MINUTE!" Roan bellowed from somewhere inside the house. There was then lots of banging and scuffling and—was that giggling? Allara didn't want to know what the poet was up to; she was sure they would invite the two of them to whatever it was if she expressed even the slightest ounce of interest.

The door creaked open ever so slightly. "Who issit?" they slurred.

"It's Allara, Ro. I have the books you asked for."

"Oh… Ohhhhh, Allara? How wonderful, you must come in!" With that, they flung open the door. "Oh, and you brought your handsome friend," they said, punctuated with a wink.

Taran stifled a laugh and shifted on his feet. It would be out of character for Roan if they didn't hit on anyone within a two-foot radius. Much to Taran's chagrin, he was often the target of their more amorous overtures.

"We really have to be going." Allara tried to look as sorry as she could manage, not that it would make much of a difference.

"Bah, you. Always such a sourpuss. Well, here's your gold, then." They fumbled around in the pockets of their velvet emerald cloak until they found their purse. A piece of lint floated to the floor as they held the stack of coins out to Allara. She scooped them into her hand and replaced them with the books she had gotten.

"Marvelous, thank you, dear. Do come again." And with that, in a blur of blonde curls and embroidered velvets, they shut the door on the pair. She could hear a slow shuffling and some grumbling, followed by raucous laughter and the return of gentle music.

"Must be some party." Taran whistled.

"Hopefully they're drunk enough that they won't remember anything tomorrow." Allara waggled her eyebrows and pulled the remaining book out from under her coat.

"Allara, you didn't!" Taran burst into a fit of laughter. "What do you want with a dingy poetry book?"

"I'll tell you after you explain where you've been all this time," she responded in a huff. Taran never kept a surprise running for this long; he knew how much she hated them.

"Roan is right. You are a sourpuss," he teased.

She brooded as she flipped the book every which way in her hands. She'd let Taran have his fun, even though she knew she shouldn't have kept the book. But Allara had made a routine of bringing her sister new little things each week. Money had slowed, first with their mother and now with the jobs scarce, but she didn't have the heart to stop getting things for her. She'd make her penance to the gods at some point. It was just nice to see Daia smile.

If the walk to Roan's was long, then the walk to Taran's was even longer. He lived on the edge of the capital, close to the docks. His family had been fishermen for as long as they could remember, so the wharf was their home. As they returned to the Middle Circle border, the sun was setting lazily in the sky, streams of orange and purple painting the clouds and casting a gentle glow over the cobblestone streets. Lanterns above the shops began to flicker on, powered by crystals that stored small bits of magic—magic of the mages, who were fewer and fewer in number each year. Sooner or later, magic would be completely gone from Averna—maybe even from the world.

They passed through the border back into the Outer Circle without a glance. Passes weren't needed to enter their circle; only the braver tourists and the common folk ever deigned to enter.

Finally, they arrived at Taran's house just as the bells chimed for the evening meal. Allara could already hear his family from the street. They rented a modest single-story house with just a few rooms. Taran and his two brothers shared a room, and his parents had a bedroom to themselves, which just left room for a kitchen and a tiny living room. His younger sisters pulled out cots in the living room each night for a bit of privacy. It wasn't much space for seven people; none of the houses in the Outer Circle were ever enough. But since they were near the water, they had a clear, beautiful view of the sea. Taran's father always said they had the biggest house in Oberon, with the ocean being their back-yard. Allara always liked the way he looked on the bright side of things. She could certainly do more of that herself.

Taran led her in through the creaky door and into a warm, lived-in space. She pretended not to notice as he ripped off the bright yellow past-due notice that had been tacked to the door, replaced so often that the city official didn't even bother to bring a new nail each time. Immediately, her nerves calmed as she crossed the threshold. Allara had spent almost as much time here as she did in her own home in their school years. Once her father had been arrested, and her mother overwhelmed between her and Daia, Allara always tried to stay busy and out of the house. Spending time at the Casilars' was the only time she wasn't getting into trouble.

Taran's sisters were in the living room with their father,

playing Kitra, a card game popular with pirates that had spread across the port cities of Averna. From the looks of things, their father was not faring well. She could hear his brothers in their bedroom, yelling and laughing. She knew them well enough to assume that they were wrestling. Taran's second-oldest brother, Saylin, had married a nice tavern girl a few years back. They shared a house near the markets now with a few other young couples. His other two brothers were also of marrying ages, but were so rowdy and free-spirited that Allara could never imagine either of them domesticating.

"Taran, is that you?" his mother called from the kitchen. The sweet smell of honey loaves wafted into the living room, and Allara's mouth involuntarily began to water. Taran's mother was the best baker next to the shop owners in Allara's neighborhood. There were some things, like her honey loaf, that even surpassed the local bakery. Not that Allara would ever admit it, for fear of her free loaves of burnt bread being revoked.

"Hey, Ma. Allara's here," Taran called as they wandered into the kitchen. It was incredibly humid from the oven's radiating heat and littered with worn recipe books and draw-ings of Taran's. His mother stood over a sheet of loaves, flour across the entire countertop and her clothes. Allara knew all that wayward flour would be carefully scooped up so as not to waste any. Mrs. Casilar was beaming as she stood amidst the chaos, and Allara felt a twinge of heartache at the sight.

"Oh, Allara, darling!" His mother stepped out from around the counter, wiping her hands on her apron. Her auburn hair was tied up in a wild bun, with ringlets floating down around her temples. She was a very slight woman, incredibly kind—though when she wanted to be, she was absolutely terrifying. "How good to see you!" She pulled

Allara in for a tight hug, strands of her curls tickling Allara's face as she leaned in.

"It's good to see you too, Mrs. Casilar." Allara smiled as she leaned back and brushed wayward flour off of her trousers. Taran's mother was a messy cook, but she said the best cooks should make a little bit of a mess. And from what Allara had tasted of her cooking, she was right.

"It feels like ages since you've joined us for dinner. We'd love to have you sometime this week."

"I'd be happy to," Allara responded. Although dinners with the Casilars were loud and a bit overwhelming, she always laughed so hard that her stomach ached.

"Yes, Ma, Allara will be over for dinner, you know she loves your food."

Allara chuckled and didn't protest, but he didn't have to make her sound like such a glutton.

Taran continued, "We'll be at the docks. Holler if you need anything." With that, he grabbed Allara's hand and dragged her out back.

They walked up to the wooden railing and leaned up against it, taking in the view. The air was brisk around her thin jacket—one that had lasted her many seasons. She glanced over at Taran, wondering why he hadn't begun some grand spiel. He was nothing if not dramatic. Instead, he was fiddling with the charm of his bracelet—a nervous tic he thought that no one noticed. Allara decided to save him the trouble.

"I hope you're intending to build suspense..."

Taran gave a dry chuckle, but didn't turn to face her.

"Taran?"

"Sorry. Just thinking."

"Well, you hardly ever do that, so it must be incredibly tiring." Still, he didn't respond to her prodding. Their bickering and teasing had gotten them through every mood or downturn the other was facing. It was their way of checking in without really saying so.

"I got into a bit of trouble. That's why I haven't been around lately."

"What? Taran—"

"Let me finish," Taran cut in, and Allara was shocked by the frankness in his expression. He looked tired. He looked like a boy who had to work day in and day out just to scrape by. But this Taran was usually hidden. She could count on one hand the number of times he had let her see him like this, and it was never good.

"I bet against myself in my last match. I had someone place it for me, but they found out anyway. I was supposed to throw the match and I'd have earned double what I would've gotten from winning. The gym's owner had his guys rough me up."

Allara's stomach dropped. She hadn't even been aware that Taran had gone back to boxing, let alone *this*.

"Taran, Gods, are you alright?"

"I'm fine, really. But I couldn't box for a while. A guy who said he was in the stands came and found me about a week later. Said he thought I'd suit a job he was putting together."

Allara hesitated. Taran was constantly trying out some new job or angle that he swore would fix things. But more often than not, Taran's leads turned out to be more trouble than they were worth. Cheap thrills and nights in a cell at best. Allara used to say yes to whatever antics he had planned. But she needed to not starve more than she needed to feel that rush again.

"What is it?" she said against her better judgment, letting her curiosity take over. She didn't have to say yes; there wasn't any harm in hearing him out. How many times had she told herself that same sentiment? It was almost comical by now.

"This is a solid job, Allara. No catch."

She crossed her arms and waited. Taran had a flair for theatrics, but his performances had stopped wooing her when they were twelve.

"This group needs a few extra for something they have planned."

"What group?" she responded dismissively.

"The Fools."

At that, Allara's gaze returned to his, studying. The Fools were a joke—always had been. Anyone who knew the name knew they'd fallen out of favor in recent months. They handled every job that was considered *unsavory*. And from what Allara knew, they'd shrank in number considerably.

"What do they want with you?" she asked, trying her best to act indifferent. If Taran sensed she was interested, he'd know he'd already won. Allara wanted to make him sweat a bit, and at least be able to find out what this gods-damned job even was.

"With *us*," he corrected.

Allara scoffed at the presumption. More than anything, she was annoyed she wasn't as convincing of an actor as he was. He knew better with her.

"And they wanted to wait 'til I had another person to give me the details."

Allara let out a humorless chuckle. "It doesn't even sound like you've been offered a job."

Taran crossed his arms over his chest, the silver charm on his yarn bracelet reflecting the moon's glow. "You say that like a little mystery is a bad thing."

"Be serious. I need a better guarantee than that."

"And you think I don't?" he countered.

"I didn't mean—"

"I get it," he cut her off.

She loosed a long breath. Out of anyone on this island, he

did get it. She knew he always had her best interests—all their best interests, really—at heart. But something about all of this didn't feel right to her. Allara used to make a habit of ignoring her conscience for fun. She found that she didn't really have that luxury anymore.

"Listen, whatever this is, Allara, the pay is good."

"How good?"

"Like, never work another odd job in your life good."

She scoffed. "That's impossible." Taran meant well, but there was no job in all of Averna that could pay that well. Especially not if there were too many hands in the pot. "What kind of crew?" Realistically, even though she wasn't *at all* considering this nonsense, she wanted to know how many ways they'd have to split the earnings.

"Six, besides us."

"What's the sum, then?"

"Eight hundred thousand gold."

That *was* quite the payout. But gold split seven ways wouldn't last forever with her sister's medicines, food, water, and heat. Allara could make an endless list of just how expensive staying alive and well truly was.

"Taran, that's not—"

"Each."

She must have had her bewilderment written on her face, because Taran cracked an obnoxiously arrogant smile. "Interested now?"

She wished she could shove him over the railing straight into his beloved ocean. Instead, she just turned outwards toward the endless expanse of the night sky.

"Moderately."

CHAPTER TWO
AUREN

His day had turned to shit remarkably fast, Auren thought as he hid in the rafters. He had been stuck in this vile warehouse for two extra hours because *someone* got the guard change wrong. Auren suspected that this was Nymm's payback for the last job they had done together. It wasn't his fault she couldn't outrun that fishmonger. Sometimes things just didn't work out. Like right now, with the way his calves burned as if they were being set on fire cell by cell. If he had known he was going to be stuck hidden away up here, he would have positioned himself more comfortably.

But nevertheless, even if he had to wait all day, this was sure to be an easy outing. They needed some information from the books that were kept in the shipping hall, so Auren just had to make copies without being seen. Even a child could be stealthy and use a bit of carbon. When Auren was given this job, he was almost offended, but he was the most senior member, and he had to set an example. Even if there was barely anyone left to set an example for.

He'd sent out offers to prospective candidates, but no one

knew anything about them. Not that it mattered much; time wasn't on their side. And as long as they weren't stupid or unbearably dull, Auren found he didn't mind. Provided that two from the bunch met their standards, then he would be satisfied.

It was always interesting seeing what kinds of people their line of work usually attracted. Only he and Nymm had stayed with their crew this long. Most left, got caught, or got killed. Auren had thus far prided himself on not achieving the latter. Though he did have some interesting scars to test the sentiment.

He was dressed in deep black leathers, which one would assume would be an added bonus for sneaking around. If anything, Auren always loved to dress the part. He did cut a rather imposing figure most days. His height had him towering above his peers in classes, marking him as a frequent target. But he was sure the boys that teased him only did so because they hated looking up at him so much. His curly chestnut hair was slicked down out of his way, making the lines of his jaw and cheekbones seem more rigid. His friends had always said he looked mean before they had gotten to know him. He just wouldn't have guessed how well that would serve him in his career.

But he'd hardly wager that he'd strike fear in anyone's heart if they saw him crumpled up in the rafters like a timid spider. He wondered how Nymm would have done this job if it had been given to her. The insufferable brat probably would have walked right through the front doors somehow and gotten away with it. But Auren knew his strengths and his weaknesses. And he definitely wasn't like Nymm. So, he took the traditional route of sneaking about, even though it now felt incredibly ridiculous.

As if fate itself knew his legs were about to give out, the last whistling guard did their round and left through the large double doors. The resounding click of the lock sounded as sweet as a hymn. Auren deftly jumped down to the floor—well, as deftly as he could manage, given his right leg had gone almost entirely numb. Not wanting to waste much time, he hobbled over to the small office buried behind the piles of shipping crates and cargo.

The warehouse was Valmaris-operated, known informally as the Pilferer's Den. All "contraband" and forfeited goods ended up there. Relics from the outlawed Civarran Saints, cases of illegally made fire wine, and banned books lined the shelves he walked through. As of late, more and more altars and statues of the Avernan gods were winding up among the confiscated goods. But outside of those relics, from before the occupation, most of the stuff was just that: stuff. If you were unlucky enough to catch the eye of the shipping guards, you could almost certainly say goodbye to some of your wares. Most items were conveniently sold back to Valmaris at a profit. He had heard of several merchants who had to go out of business from being so regularly targeted by the port guards.

Auren suddenly didn't feel bad as he *accidentally* knocked various books into his satchel as he walked by. He picked the lock on the office door and pushed his way inside, careful to keep track of his timing. He began sifting through all the files on the desk and the cabinets below, until he found the transport ledgers for the ship he was tasked to find: *Conqueror's Glory*. Auren rolled his eyes at the Valmaran lack of subtlety. He wasn't sure what in the world this had to do with their current gig, but he wasn't the type to ask questions.

He quickly smoothed the sheet of carbon over the pages and began steadily applying pressure to the parchment he placed on top. This process created perfect transfers of the documents underneath, all without leaving a trace. Insultingly simple, but he would be in and out in less than the allotted time. He gave the last transfer one final swipe to make sure there weren't any missing details, then replaced everything how he had found it. Honestly, he was a bit out of practice with this part, so he hoped any differences were indistinguishable enough.

The front door would be locked and awaiting the next guard, so he had to go back out the way he came: through the roof. Luckily for him, the crates and packages were haphazardly stacked high enough that all he'd have to do was make one good jump. This was always the fun part for him. Auren made sure the transfers were securely strapped in his satchel and began scrambling up the side of the tallest set of shelves. Judging by the sound of them as they swayed beneath him, they were filled with bottles of liquid.

He shifted his weight when he got to the more precariously stacked crates on top. They groaned in protest as he ambled up them. As he reached for the last crate, he found the lid was not properly secured, and it tumbled down to the floor. Auren flailed about, looking for a place to find purchase. He remembered his nonstop drills with Nymm, to be quick and analyze the situation; it was a bodily memory at this point to stop his fall on the protruding edge of a crate farther down.

Auren slowly made his way back up, hoping no one would think twice about the racket he had made. Though it seemed at least his luck had improved as he prepared to make the leap onto the opening to the roof—and found the uppermost crate to be filled with spirits. It wasn't a kind he preferred, but then again, anything free always tasted a bit sweeter to him. He'd happily drink old stable water if it meant sticking it to someone in charge of this shithole city.

"You smell like sewage," Nymm said upon his return, crinkling her hooked nose in disgust.

"You're well acquainted with it, then?" Auren smirked and tossed the transfers her way. The Guild was all-hands-on-deck, but if anyone was the resident spymaster, it was Nymm. She traded secrets the way lords traded idle gossip over tea. Not that he would ever admit it to her or anyone else, but Auren was always impressed by Nymm. She looked about four years younger than a woman of twenty-six, but was an absolute terror. Nymm was clever and cold when she had to be—which was almost always. He wasn't sure if what she had earned was respect, but it was a hell of a lot better than any alternative she would have had, especially as a Civarran. She was something of a leader to the Guild, partly because of how long she had been with them, but mostly because she deserved it.

Auren needed a wash, and he hoped that the solar canisters had been refilled. Lately, someone had been making a bad habit of using up all the warm water and "forgetting" to set the canisters outside to warm more. Everyone else had to use regular (and incredibly chilly) river water. If he had any guess about the culprit, it'd be that brute of a bouncer, Virgil. He had a permanent sneer on his face and the unfortunate personality to match. If he weren't the largest and meanest-looking person Auren had ever seen, he would've made the case to let him go. But as much as Auren hated to admit it, he'd rather have that nasty fool working with him than against him. Even if he did hog all the warm water.

Auren reached his room on the second floor and threw himself down on the bed. It was so early when he'd started the job that the day had really only just begun by the second bell. It was pathetic for him to be so exhausted when a full day lay ahead. Still, he gave in to temptation and closed his eyes. He counted down from ten, planning to get back up once he reached zero.

The next thing he knew, the sun was sitting across his eyes, waking him. Auren groaned as he stretched his sore legs out. All the hot water would certainly be gone by now. He sat up and leaned against the wall running along the bed. His room was rather small, fitting a single bed, a desk, and a chest for his belongings. But it was his own room, unlike the one he'd had to share with four other boys when he had first joined up. Once he'd made it clear he wasn't going to be gotten rid of, he was given a room on the second floor. It was unofficially the floor for those who were permanent fixtures in their operation.

He hadn't arrived with much when he was recruited for his first job, but he had gathered all sorts of odds and ends in the time since. Little trophies like gemstone brooches and pretty silver quills lined his desk among the collection of worn, mismatched books. It was going to be twelve years soon enough.

He had been sixteen years old when he got into a bad fight. Kids in his class had been picking on him per usual, but that time, one of them had made a comment about his sister. If they had had any sense, they would have realized no one said anything about his sister and left with all of their bones the way they were supposed to be. Turned out that one of the boys was the son of a guard captain, and he had taken great offense when Auren broke both his wrists and his nose. He'd been in enough fights even at that age that he knew where to hit to really make it hurt.

They took him in for a fortnight or so, and when he got out, his mother said there was no place in her house for a screw-up like him. So, he'd bounced around from sleeping on park benches to sleeping under bridges. He'd sneak into the garden and visit his sister through the window most nights, until all of a sudden, she stopped leaving it unlatched. Out of everything he'd ever done—every scrap he'd gotten into, every safe he'd robbed—nothing kept him awake at night like that locked window.

Auren sighed and stretched his neck back and forth. It was bad enough he had spent half his morning posed like a crumpled-up piece of parchment, and his bed did him no favors. He supposed it was time to get back up, despite feeling anything but well rested. He needed to scrounge around the kitchen before all the leftovers from breakfast were taken too.

He hoped Ilia had saved something for him. She made the best eggs in the capital. Nymm always teased him for saying so, but the fact was that they were perfectly scrambled every time—not dry, like most people made them, and not too runny either. People in their line of work didn't normally have an appreciation for food like Auren did. As long as they didn't starve, it was good enough for them. But he had always enjoyed experimenting with techniques and flavors when he could. He and Ilia always traded recipes; it was nice to talk about something other than work. Apart from Nymm, being in the Guild was really all he had in common with anyone else in the house.

He lumbered down to the first floor, jumping past the last three steps. The second step from the bottom always tilted under any weight, leading to many bruises and broken bones throughout the years. It was almost an initiation in and of itself to see how many times the new recruits would stumble over it before they wised up. Nymm was the only person light-footed enough to use it without toppling over. She had tried to teach him in the past, but Auren was too heavy to do anything but clomp around. She always scoffed after their lessons like it was a bad thing. Maybe to her, it was. Auren's style was more direct, to say the least.

Recruits didn't receive any sort of official training, but over the years, certain long-standing members had taken it upon themselves to instruct on certain skill sets informally. Auren was unbeatable in most areas of combat, so he tried to teach morning training to anyone who bothered to show up. Nymm knew the best ways to sneak about, pick locks, and pilfer without leaving a trace. Her preferred method of teaching was practical: simulations and lessons in the field. Their oldest recruit, Tulvar, knew the best recipes for potions and poisons. They made sure that all members carried a travel kit of the basics—poultices for open wounds, antidotes for common poisons, and potions for all kinds of ailments. Auren was on their good side, so they usually made him a few draughts for hangover cures as well.

The Guild's reputation had started off as the punch line to every joke in the underworld. A gaggle of orphans and runaways wasn't supposed to be good for anything. But over the next few years, they had proven that they were good for more than just the odd job. Members had a knack for making things disappear in one place and reappear in an entirely new one. Safes were never secure, secrets were never kept, and debts were paid. Those who gave them jobs in the early days were mocked as fools. So, they became The Fools' Guild as a sort of reversal. Now, they were on par with The Shades and The Peddlers, the other pillars of their little underworld. If someone needed a problem solved outside of the law, one of the guilds would have the means to help them—for a price, of course.

The Fools had somewhat fallen from grace over the past few months. Their last few jobs had gone off so poorly that if Auren hadn't been there himself, he would have claimed there was sabotage involved. Word of mouth was all a guild had to build their reputation. With the downturn, the jobs came fewer and fewer, and most of their number moved on. There were only eight of them left, when they should be up to at least triple that number to run things effectively.

Even at that number, Ilia and Tulvar already rarely worked in the field. It was agreed upon that they handle the more behind-the-scenes responsibilities of a functioning guild. But if things continued as they were, or the potential new hires didn't work out, they might not have much of a choice. Everyone had to earn their keep somehow.

Now, they had finally landed a job that would get them back to the way things had been. The job was so big that it required new members and had the biggest payout Auren had ever heard of in underworld history. As long as they didn't screw it up, they would all be legends. Auren could earn enough to prove to his family that he had made something out of himself.

Maybe it would be enough that he could finally go home.

He walked into the drafty kitchen and saw a plate with two stuffed rolls still left out. He sent a small thanks to Ilia for fending off those who would have undoubtedly wanted seconds. Since the jobs had become less prolific, so had the pay—and their meager crew had all gained room in their waistbands over the spring. The roll was speckled with bits of fresh rosemary, one of Auren's favorites. He would have to properly thank Ilia when he saw her next.

After he'd had his roll, he cleaned up and set the remaining pastry in the frost box to keep things fresh. The house was empty, with Nymm on to her part of the job and the rest of the recruits preparing for their candidates' trials. That meant a lot of free time, which Auren usually enjoyed. But he had endured far too much free time as of late. He had read and reread all of the books in his expansive collection and even began a new arrow design. But without the gold for some supplies he needed, that project was at a standstill. Auren longed for the days when he woke with a defined purpose. Guild life wasn't for every manner of person, but he craved the structure. If he was being honest with himself, he enjoyed being told what to do, what jobs to take, and more or less how to do them. Auren found that the less power was in his hands, the less stupid decisions he was bound to make.

So, he decided to sharpen what was in their armory and wait for Nymm to return. He savored the routine of grinding the blades and arrows on the stone at just the right angle. It required enough focus that his mind wandered to little else. People in their line of work needed something for themselves to take the edge off. Auren had a handful of rituals to keep his thoughts at bay. Smithing, tinkering, and cooking were his favorites at the moment, although his tastes were known to change. He'd had a phase of drinking, like most new recruits, and he had slept his way through half of the Outer Circle before it all caught up to him. Auren had seen enough friends chase away their darkness by burning themselves in the flames, and he'd be damned if he let that be his end too.

CHAPTER THREE
NYMM

The look on Auren's face that morning had been so worth it. It had been weeks since their last job, and Nymm still couldn't go down to the docks without getting the evil eye from half the crews. Not that she cared what anyone thought, per se, but she had always been superstitious about bad energy. She got it from her mother, who had always crossed her heart and knocked on wood after every ambiguous phrase … for all the good that did her. But some habits were harder to shake than others, and it comforted Nymm to still have a small bit of her mother in her.

Maybe the wiser thing would have been to make herself scarce until after Auren calmed down, but Nymm had not felt particularly wise that morning. In fact, she thought she'd rather delight in the look on his face when he saw her. If only she could have seen his expression when he realized how she'd fibbed with the guard schedule. He wouldn't have been that mad anyway; if anything, he'd probably expected her reprisal.

Now, though, Nymm knew she'd have time before he

woke from his nap, so she thought to go out and get him a peace offering—just in case. Auren had an insatiable taste for spicy foods, and his favorite snack was the capital's famous suppli—round little rice balls cooked in a red pepper sauce. There was a little shop that made them better than anyone else in the capital, but they always sold out by the third bell. Luckily for her, it was still early enough, and the stand was also on the way to the next part of their mysterious new job.

She fastened her lightest black cloak around her matching tunic and slipped on her favorite pair of boots. She had a habit of always dressing like she was up to no good, even for the most innocent of tasks. She shoved her coin purse into a pocket of her satchel, trying to ignore the catch in her chest from how light it felt. If their fixer was right about this new job, then they were on the brink of unimaginable wealth and reward. She just had to hope it was a *when* and not an *if*.

She left the warehouse she'd called home for the better part of ten years and joined the bustle of the early morning. There was something exciting about being out in town this early, and Nymm felt an odd sense of purpose. She smelled freshly baked bread wafting out of open windows. Stray dogs and cats drank from kindly offered bowls or divots in the cobblestones where the morning dew had collected. The day was so alive with possibilities, and it hadn't been soured by anything yet.

What was hard to ignore, however, was the increasing number of people hanging out of alleyways and shop doors, covered in rags or what little they owned. With the festival less than two weeks away, it seemed the city guard had begun the Sweep, pushing all the "undesirables" toward the Outer Circle and away from the naive eyes of incoming visitors. Where they expected all these people to go was a mystery, though Nymm suspected that if there were a way to magic it so, they'd have them all vanish and be done with it.

She tried not to see her family in the dark, sad eyes of the children crouched under awnings or the tousled umber hair of women bent down to wash themselves aimlessly. It was more than likely that some of them were her people, bits of home. She could never forget her past, would never want to, but deep down, there was a nasty urge to be better than them. She wouldn't give the citizens of the capital anything to look down on when it came to her. They could say what they wanted about her line of work, her demeanor. But they couldn't deny that she'd come a long way from being one of those forgotten refugees that littered the cobblestone streets.

The carbon transfers Auren had made were burning a hole in her pocket. She had looked them over twice after he had given them to her, but she couldn't read the Valmaran. She cursed herself for not learning the language better. She hadn't attended a fancy Oberon school like Auren and the others, where Valmaris's influence grew with each year. She hadn't received formal schooling for most of her childhood, actually, but she got on just fine.

Nymm reached the market and lined up for the stall with the bright red banners and the longest wait. But the saints must have been on her side, as the line wasn't half as long as it usually was. When it was her turn, she placed an order for the large portion to go, so it came in a fancy solar canister to keep the heat for longer. The carnelian crystal embedded in the lid glowed a deep red as it transmitted the small magic.

Her next stop chewed at her heels as she walked, though her stride never faltered. This was the part of being in charge that she liked the least, but someone had to get their hands dirty, and that someone almost always happened to be her. Besides the decrease in jobs they'd been offered, contracts had been taken out from under them, payments had been lower than expected, and large numbers of their guild were leaving with suspicious regularity.

Téo had been their recruiter for the past three seasons, and each season, their circumstances were more and more dire. Auren, saints bless him, argued that it was just poor luck. But Nymm knew better. She had realized as Téo brought in new members on his word, letting them skip initiation and join blind, that something was amiss. They got put on the best jobs and left just as quickly. And Nymm could never find big discrepancies in the books, but there were little ones—payouts split slightly off, or goods delivered missing one or two items.

It was bad enough that the other guilds were against them—that was just the cutthroat nature of the underworld —but they couldn't be working against themselves too. So, it was well past time Téo was handled. She only hoped that he didn't fight her on it, because doing so would mean consequences Nymm was not ready to accept.

The tavern she entered was dense, dark, and humid. Bodies were packed tightly into the space, and the stone floor glistened with spilled ale from rowdy patrons and off-balance servers. The fourth bell had rung during her walk, and with everyone having their morning meal, there wasn't a spare table or chair to be found. Nymm squeezed her way through the small gaps she could find in the mass of patrons, heading toward a door in the back, just off to the side of the bar. A tall, lanky man stood against the wall next to it, arms crossed and one leg propped up on the uneven stone wall. Nymm nodded, and he opened the door.

The raucous sounds of the tavern faded away as he shut it behind her. She closed her eyes and took in one small breath before schooling her face into a cold, hard mask. Just past the small entryway, a large wooden table sat under the warm light of a massive lantern hanging from the ceiling. Eight people sat around the perimeter, holding cards at eye level.

Strewn about the table were flagons of ale, gems, gold

coins, and small slips of parchment—guild contracts. It was against the Fixer Guild's policy to wager with contracts, but that didn't stop some of the more unscrupulous members of the underworld from betting jobs when they lacked the funds otherwise. It was weak to fold out of a game. You played until you won, or had nothing left to lose.

Nymm had turned a blind eye to Téo's betting habits, especially as they'd had less and less jobs as of late. Getting work by any means was better than no work at all. But it only took one conversation a few months ago with her friend Shae, of the Fixer Guild, to find that jobs they'd been assigned were being completed by other guilds. Téo had been betting their contracts, and losing.

Téo's back was to Nymm when she entered, and she kept to the ring of shadows outside of the lantern's glow. His broad shoulders were drawn in, from concentration or defeat, Nymm wasn't sure, as the light bounced off his tawny skin and sandy hair. He had no idea she was here. In fact, none of the players saw her as she lingered at the edge of the room. She thought to eavesdrop a bit, but they were talking of another guild's—The Peddlers'— recent scandal. Their guild master, a smarmy man Nymm had never liked, had run off with most of the guild's profits, meant to be split, invested, and saved for expenses. He'd taken two lovers and six of the chests in the middle of the night. It seemed The Fools weren't the only ones with internal issues.

But Nymm had other work to do and had no interest in gossip, especially what she already knew. She drew out of the shadows silently, and Téo did not turn, but the rest of the players facing her direction grew wide-eyed and white-faced. Her reputation never seemed to fail her when she needed it. Téo, glancing at the other players' expressions, turned his neck to find Nymm there, and dropped his cards face-up on the table.

Nymm walked closer, leaning over his shoulder, almost intimately. She clucked her tongue. "You're far too bold for such a poor hand, Téo." His collection of gold and parchment had been slipped toward the center of the table, his remaining horde laughably small.

Without her needing to instruct them, the rest of the players rose from the table and left the room, the sound of their chairs scraping against the stone floor echoing in the empty space.

Téo laughed, but it was a brittle, hollow sound. "Had you wanted to play, Nymm? That's too bad; it seems our game has ended."

Nymm settled into the chair on his left, resting her feet on the table's edge. She leaned back just so that her cloak fell away, revealing the two silver daggers strapped to her thigh.

Téo's throat worked against its tension. "You came all the way down here for me? I feel so special."

"Enough quips, Téo." She let the guise fall just a bit, drawing her legs back down to the ground so she could lean in toward him. "You've been double-crossing us. Why?"

His eyebrows shot up toward his hairline. "I would never double on you, honest. How could you think that?"

"We've lost half our contracts, and even more than that in numbers. You think it's a coincidence?"

His eyes drew down into his lap. "I think you're misunderstanding the situation."

"If you think I don't have my own contacts, you'd be wrong." She tilted her head, like a predator assessing its prey. "Do you think me a true fool?"

"Gods, no. But there must be some other explanation." He let out a shaky breath. "I admit, things have been ... difficult for us lately. But I'm doing everything I can to help. You have to believe that."

"Unfortunately for you, I don't." She tossed down a

contract that had been marked with The Fools' crest—a comedy mask and a tragedy mask reversed—and had been stamped over with the inky crest of The Shades. "How many contracts have you cost us?"

"What? No, Nymm, I—"

"A number, Téo. I won't ask again."

"Nine. This season."

"And the rest?"

His silence hung heavy in the air. "I don't know."

She sat back in her chair, letting her posture drop. She'd known the answer for weeks now; him saying it changed nothing. But still, nausea settled into her gut. They were a guild, a family. You weren't supposed to do things like this to your own family. Still, Téo wasn't a bad person, just an incredibly selfish one.

He read her expression. He did know her well enough, it seemed. "Are you going to kill me?"

Nymm laughed. "Kill you? No. I won't commit that kind of sin for you. You're not worth it. But…" She unsheathed the dagger at her thigh. "… I will ensure you never try to take another guild down with you."

Her strikes were quick, brutal. He didn't even have the time to flinch. The X under his left eye bloomed crimson before it began to trickle down his cheek like a tear.

"Good luck finding work now, Téo. If I ever hear your name spoken to me again, I will come back. I don't care what the saints or the gods may think."

To his credit, he was stoic. He bore the mark and the pain of it with dignity. But that would not help him—not now, marked as a traitor to his own people. If there was no law, no conscience in the underworld, then it would collapse under its own treachery. There had to be a line for all of them. Even if it blurred from time to time, it still had to exist somewhere.

She stalked out of the back room and through the crowded tavern. She was in and out before the bells had even changed. The streets outside were frenzied with people going between the morning meal and work. Vendors hawked their goods from narrow alleyway openings, and guards patrolled past in rigid marches. With the festival approaching, there were the obvious tourists, naive in coming to the Outer Circle at all. She could already spot the pickpockets and scammers in the crowd, marking their targets. It was all too much.

Nymm turned a corner and headed down an alley, shadowed by the height of the surrounding buildings. She leaned against the cold, worn stone to try to catch her breath. Her parents hadn't raised her to be cruel, unforgiving. It felt like her heart was squeezing shut with the ache that wracked it. What would they think if they could see her now, like this? And Téo... He was funny, outrageous. She didn't know what course he'd be set on with no way to join another guild. But that was the way things had to be done. Life had made her this way. Be cruel, or cruelties were cast upon you. Nymm knew that truth firsthand.

So, she straightened up and rolled her shoulders. There was still more work to do.

S he reached her destination, The Valmaris Vault, via the rooftops, giving herself the best vantage point to scout things out and avoid having to go through the border inspection.

There were more guards in the Middle Circle than the Outer, but she knew the things they usually looked for. The alley across from her looked incredibly tight, but Nymm was pleased, as that would work to her advantage. The guards all seemed to be stationary too, so no chance of them happening upon her once she got started. Yet again, she was grateful for the ineptitude of their local officials.

She decided to be as straightforward as possible to save time, shimmying down the drainpipe along the back corner of the bank. She landed in a crouch and scanned the length of the building. Supposedly, there would be a loose brick to slip the transfers behind until they were collected by whomever they were working for. They all looked surprisingly uniform, so she resorted to rapping on some with her knuckles. Hopefully, the false space behind would make some sort of sound. She started with the bricks at her crouched height, choosing ones she'd have picked if she had created this system. From there, she went up and down, left and right, in a small grid, so she wouldn't lose her place.

After her fiftieth guess or so, she heard a brisk echo of hollowness and pried it from the wall. She rolled the pages together and filed them into the empty space, replacing the brick when she was done.

Nymm headed out of the alley and onto the street, matching her stride with the flow of traffic so as not to draw attention to herself. Luckily, that had gone off as easily as she had hoped, but her doubts had only grown. So far, the tasks they had been given were just as ordinary as the work they normally did. It certainly wasn't worth the payout they were being promised. It was against the rules to ask a fixer who the customer was, or any identifying details, but Nymm wished she knew their contractor's motivations. She put aside those thoughts for the time being, and knew that if need be, she could bring them up to Auren. For all their bickering and pranks, they truly did have each other's backs most in the Guild.

With that task done, all there was to do was wait, which was Nymm's least favorite endeavor. She knew Auren would be just as miserable as her, so she hoped she could persuade him to help her with chores in the meantime. For having lived on his own for the longest, Auren was incredibly lazy with housekeeping. If he wasn't living with others, he'd probably be living in a pigsty. Nymm smiled to herself, thinking of how her sisters used to tease her for being the same way. It had been a long time since those days, and in the years since, she had learned a tremendous amount of discipline. But her heart always ached with something like fondness when she teased Auren for the same thing. The twinge of sadness was never far behind the smile.

When Nymm arrived back home, it was much livelier than it had been when she'd left. The kitchen was littered with glass jars and vials in all manner of shapes and sizes as Tulvar and Ilia worked around each other. Ilia's steps were uneven as she moved about the narrow kitchen. Auren had taken a look at her prosthetic, but couldn't find the cause of her imbalance. Truthfully, she probably needed a new one entirely, but that required gold she didn't have.

Tulvar muttered something quietly, and Ilia laughed, then they moved quickly to pour a thick mixture into a boiling pot before dropping in some herbs from a vial slowly. Ilia stirred for them between mixing whatever was in her own pot. Being one-handed, Tulvar had workarounds for most everything, but they always said alchemy was an art of timing as much as science. Sometimes, an extra pair of hands was needed.

The fragrances of poultices battled for air space with whatever stew Ilia was preparing for dinner. As of late, they didn't have enough gold to provide a midday meal, so most often it was skipped. She knew the suppli would be doubly appreciated by Auren to hold him over until evening.

The two newer recruits were lazing about the living space

filled with worn and mismatched furniture. They both avoided Nymm's eyes and gave her a wide berth as she stalked through the warehouse. She figured Auren might be out back with the makeshift armory they had accumulated due to his recent interest. Not that Nymm would complain; it never hurt to be well stocked for the line of work they were in.

Around the back of their warehouse-turned-home, they'd created a tiny blacksmith forge and arms storage in the alleyway they called their backyard. The Outer Circle was so cramped with buildings that no one had space beyond their four walls. But they couldn't have the forge indoors, and a lot of blacksmiths didn't want the trouble of being on the guards' radar for selling to an underworld guild. So, they had taken over the space of the alleyway that ran behind their building, and if anyone was foolish enough to steal from them, then they wouldn't be making the same mistake twice.

She found Auren hunched over the worktable off to the side of the forge, littered with a handful of throwing and sheath knives. They were sharpened to a lethal point, but Auren still went over them back and forth with oil and a stone to make sure they were perfect. For having the appearance of a brutish rogue, he had a much finer touch than one would guess. He glowered at her when she loomed over his shoulder. Most people Nymm could sneak up on; whether she still got the jump on Auren or he just humored her, she wasn't certain.

She held out the canister with the suppli. "I come in peace."

He scowled, but took the canister from her carefully. "I suppose you're forgiven."

Nymm's laugh was internal as he tore off the lid and popped a skewered rice ball in his mouth, steam still rising into the air, despite the hours that had passed. She let him eat as she wrapped the base of the arrowheads with fabric so they could be dipped in Tulvar's fire solution later. Once he was finished, he set the container down, and Nymm sat on the bench.

"You're back early."

Nymm just shrugged, and Auren hesitated before continuing, "And Téo?"

"It's taken care of."

"You didn't—"

"You don't truly want to know, Auren."

"Fine." He shifted. "You didn't have to do that alone, you know. I'll watch your back."

"I know."

"So … job go okay?" He wiped the bright red fire sauce off the corner of his mouth with his tongue.

"No trouble. But something feels … off."

Auren tilted his head, waiting for her to continue.

"Doesn't it feel too easy?"

"And that's a bad thing?" He chuckled.

"It's a lot of gold, Auren." She worried her bottom lip between her teeth. "And the work isn't adding up to the cost."

Auren sighed. "I wish I could tell you that you're worrying too much."

"But you agree?"

"I do." His mouth set in a hard line. There were more creases between his brows than there had been when she'd first met him. Their line of work had a much earlier expiration date than most occupations. The stress always aged them.

"I don't want to jinx things, but—"

"You and your superstitions."

She rolled her eyes. "You'll mock me until you see that

I'm right. There are forces at work we shouldn't pretend to understand."

At that, his mouth turned down. "As ever, you may be right. But as for the job, I think we need to be smart. Hopefully, there's nothing to worry about, and we'll be paid like kings to do the work we're used to."

Nymm just nodded and left him to his tools. Auren was one of the few people who respected her opinion on matters and actually listened to her. But in this, Nymm knew she'd be alone. Auren wasn't a leader; he didn't want to give orders, just follow them. It was why she'd so easily risen to lead the Guild once her predecessor passed. By all rights, Auren was the oldest and longest-standing member, but he just had a nonchalance to him. It used to drive Nymm to wits' end, how he could be so passive, though over time, it became clear that that was who he was. If anything, it made her leadership that much smoother.

But Nymm only dealt in certainty, and she wouldn't leave such a large sum of gold up to chance. She needed to figure out this job before it got the better of them.

CHAPTER FOUR
ALLARA

It was barely past the first evening bell, and it had already been too long of a day. Allara had been to the community board in her neighborhood and three others, but had found no work. Only missing persons ads and other pleas remained, but the guard never looked at the boards. Most notices remained from several seasons prior, sun-worn and tattered.

Allara had tried getting another job from Roan, but she hadn't heard from them since she dropped off the books. In her desperation, she'd gone to their house around midday and knocked for ages, with no response. She'd even planned to pay for the book she stole and beg for forgiveness, but that wasn't the cause of their silence. Their neighbors hadn't seen them in the past week either. Allara was sure they were either entertaining or locked in their study with a quill and parchment, and would have a job for her once they reemerged. But that held no guarantee, and Allara needed more immediate ways of earning gold.

Taran's promises from that night could fix things—if they didn't get themselves killed first.

Her feet dragged as she padded through she and her sister's one-room house to the hearth, sparking a flint and holding it against the wood logs in the stone chamber. She gathered the herbs that had been drying and picked up the last glass vial sitting on the shelf—a vial that cost nearly as much as their rent. Carefully, she crushed the herbs with a pestle and dropped in the precise dosage of medication, eyeing the bottle against the flames licking in the hearth. There were two more doses left, and then she'd need to buy more. The mixture smelled putrid, and Allara was sure it tasted worse, but Daia never complained. She left the hearth burning even as she glanced at the dwindled reserve of logs sitting beside it.

In their bed—though Allara rarely slept in it anymore—Daia shivered under the worn blankets, her brows creased even in sleep. She shared Allara's bronze skin and dark hair, but she was so much duller, the spark of their heritage battered by illness and immobility. It hurt to look at her, but it hurt worse to be away, with Allara wondering if one day she'd come home to find that Daia was gone too.

Allara eased herself onto the edge of the bed, smoothing over the blanket, the last one their mother had made before she left them—left them with bills, and worry, and shame. She ran her fingers over the wrinkles in Daia's forehead, easing them back down.

Slowly, her eyes cracked open, milky as if morning mist covered the jade irises. "Allara?"

At the croak of her voice, Allara shot back up for a cup of water. "Morning, Dee." She dipped into the bucket that sat beside the door, a sodalite crystal embedded in the rim for purification. "Time for your dose."

"It's been a week already? Gods, each day seems to blur together."

Each day spent in bed, nothing to see or do, and with only

Allara for meager company. It made her want to fall to the side of their bed and wail.

As Allara turned back to her with water, she tried to infuse enthusiasm into each word. "Well, once we're done, I can read a bit more of your new book to you, if you'd like." She returned to the edge of the bed and tilted the cup toward Daia's lips. "Open."

Daia swallowed in small gulps, nodding once she was finished. "I adored that last poem."

Allara scoffed. "You like everything romantic."

"Who wouldn't?" Daia sighed dreamily.

Allara rolled her eyes, but chided herself for not watching her tone. Stories and dreams were all Daia had; it wasn't her fault the world hadn't jaded her like it had Allara. She wouldn't deny her whatever joy she was able to still have.

"Alright, another poem it is. Maybe two, if you don't start snoring in the middle."

Daia giggled, then sobered. "You'll stay until I fall back asleep?"

Allara grabbed the medication and poured it into the drained water cup. "Of course."

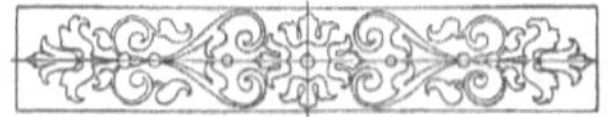

Allara flipped a gold piece in her hand over and over with the cadence of the ocean's tide. Taran had said to meet at the docks after the last bell, so they could walk to the warehouse together. If it were anyone other than Taran who had asked, she wouldn't have gone at all. She'd slipped her forged pass into her bag, along with a lockpick kit, bandages, and a knife. She had no idea what they should be prepared for, but it couldn't be anything good.

She only hoped they'd let them both leave at the end of the night.

Allara was determined not to take the job, no matter how good the pay was. She could admit she was initially swayed to the idea, but no amount of gold was worth getting killed for. Whatever the job was, it was most likely above her skill level. And if the payout was any indication of the danger, then it was too high. With work like that, you had to be good, or you would be dead. And Allara couldn't leave her sister alone. But she also needed medication, food, and everything else, and that was the insidious thought at the back of her mind that strapped on her boots and urged her to go and consider the work.

The unfortunate reality was that the further you worked from the law, the more you got paid. One could have a sense of morality, or have enough money to eat; there wasn't room enough for both.

The docks were near empty, ominous in their stillness. A guard stood at the far end to the left of where Allara leaned against the railing, but made no move to come near her. As long as Taran didn't take much longer, then they should be content to leave her alone, but the longer she stayed out past the bells, the more attention she would draw. Her pass was a very good counterfeit—she'd made it herself—but she didn't like to use it if it could be avoided. She'd tried to dress casually enough to blend in too: a loose gray shirt and black pants tucked into her only pair of boots. She'd thrown on a navy coat so as not to look too morose. It wasn't that she expected the notorious Fools' Guild to give a care as to how she dressed, but Allara always found she did better when she imagined she was playing a part. It wasn't *Allara* who was risking she and her sister's safety by considering taking an underworld job. It was someone bolder than she was, less reserved—someone whom things worked out much better for.

Footsteps sounded above the crashing of the waves, quicker than Taran's usual careless pace. He must have felt sorry for making her wait in the cold by herself. She turned slowly, tucking the gold piece back into her bag while rolling her eyes. "It's about time, Taran. I know you're not one for punctuality, but with—"

Except it wasn't Taran at all. The *feeling* rushing through her veins was that this person was a stranger, and they didn't exactly mean her harm. But they were going to hurt her anyway.

She saw flashes of black clothing, slicked-back hair, and a gloved hand rapidly approaching her temple. She tried to duck out of the way, but was struck in the shoulder, sending her careening down to the right. She grunted at the harsh yet precise impact to her joint. The pain smarted and spread all the way down to the tips of her fingers that rested against the damp wood.

"Hey!" the guard called from the end of the dock, too far away to do her any good. Allara pulled herself up from the dock, swiping out with her left leg on the ascent. Her attacker must have noticed the way she shifted her balance and had no trouble sidestepping her attempt. Her wrist ached where she'd caught herself on her fall, and her neck was starting to throb. He might have hit a pressure point—or maybe she was just too weak from malnutrition.

Where was Taran? She tried to clear her mind and focus on incapacitating her attacker enough to get away. She'd never taken defense classes or joined a club to fight. Kids like her didn't get to join the guard or the navy, so why bother? But she was a woman in the poorest district of the most populated city on the island, so she'd picked up some skills along the way. Taran and his brothers had tried to teach her basic self-defense, but it seemed their lessons didn't adhere enough for her to actually put it into practice.

Allara tried swinging wildly, listening for the sound of footsteps that would mean the guard had finally arrived. Each attempt by her was swatted away from the man as if he were dissuading a fly. She wanted to scream in frustration—and she might have, because the man had started to laugh— honest to gods laughter right in her face as he tried to rob her or do whatever it was he planned to do.

All of a sudden, as if he were tired of humoring her, he went on the offensive, knocking her arms with real force and pushing her back away from the multicolored lanterns that hung above the rails of the dock. He moved too fast for her to track, and it was clear he really had been toying with her. The next time he aimed for her temple, she had no chance of dodging it, and she crumpled to the dock before everything went dark.

When Allara opened her eyes again, she was indoors. She couldn't help the swell of panic that burst through her at the unfamiliar location and the knowledge that her hands and feet were bound. Her head ached, but she felt alert enough; it seemed her attacker knew just how hard to hit her to knock her out, but not cause a concussion or permanent damage.

She was none too proud to admit how afraid she was, but more than anything, she worried she'd never be free—that whoever had taken her wouldn't let her go. Her mind drifted to Daia. Would anyone think to check on her if Allara never made it home? They had no family left, no friends. People in the neighborhood tried their best to look out for one another, but life was hard enough tending to one's own needs. How many days would pass before anyone realized their door remained untouched? Until the aloe in the windowsill wilted away? Until the mail and notices sat in a high enough pile out of their box...? It was too dark a thought to consider.

The room was small and dank. A single table sat along the wall directly across from her, and a lamp flickered weakly above the center of the floor. She waited and waited—probably longer than necessary—until she accepted that no one was coming for her yet. That was fine. She had no intention of sticking around for whatever they had planned.

Easing side to side, she rocked the chair she was bound to until it teetered over, pain running along every part of her body that connected with the floor. She took a deep breath and listened for anyone who might have been alerted to the noise she made, and when she was certain the coast was clear, she rose up onto her knees. It was awkward to manage with the chair strapped along her back like a cloak, but she made it up on the fourth try.

Allara braced herself before throwing all of her weight onto her back, cringing when the echo of splintering wood bounced around the empty space. This time, she did hear footsteps, barely audible over the hammering of her heart and the blood rushing past her ears. With her legs still bound, she crawled to the corner of the room behind where the door would open, hoping it wouldn't smack into her when it reached the wall.

A heavy gait reached the door, and it cracked open slowly, allowing Allara to scramble behind it and out of sight.

"Hey! She's out!"

Laughter and jeers rang out after the man's announcement, and Allara's stomach sank. She'd heard the rumors; everyone in the Outer Circle had. It was known that the nobility and Inner Circle members sometimes looked to unconventional means of *entertainment*. Once they bored of the court mages and theater shows, they turned to crueler pastimes.

Her resolve had been hardened the second she came to, but there was no doubt now that she had to get out before someone caught her. Her instincts screamed that she would not get a second chance to escape.

The door shut, the click of it meeting the frame lingering in the silence. First, she wrestled with her bindings. The one around her hands had been tethered to the chair, solving that problem when she smashed it on the floor, but her ankles were providing more trouble. The knot was tight, and her fingers ached as they tried to find a bit of leeway to pull.

She was unsuccessful and wasting too much time. Instead, she scooted over to the splinters of the chair and found one sharp enough to saw through the rope. Beads of sweat dripped down from her temples and upper lip, but she didn't pause her work to wipe it away. Mercifully, the rope frayed enough for her to shimmy it over her ankles, and she bolted upright, head swimming with the sudden motion.

But a new problem already stood in her way. There were no windows to climb out of, no vents in the ceiling, and the ceiling was ridiculously high. All that was at her disposal was a bit of rope, a broken chair, and a small wooden table that was too low to give much of an advantage.

She looked back at the table, the thick legs about the length and width of her arm, and got to work breaking one off—which was much easier in her head than it was in practice. She ended up kicking it repeatedly until it broke off in a jagged shard. She just needed something to wield and fool herself into thinking she stood a chance.

She eased the door open with no resistance; they hadn't even bothered to lock it. Allara crept down the hall, mindful of the way her boots met the worn wooden floor. She paused every few steps in an attempt to listen for activity, but the pulse in her ears drowned nearly everything out. She made it to the end of the long hallway, where there was a door on each side. No light bled through the frames of either; she'd just have to guess.

Allara tried to calm her nerves and tap into her sense— that otherworldly thing that she'd spent so many years trying to ignore. After a few deep breaths, she waited, reaching deep into her gut for any kind of feeling. Warmth sluiced through her veins when she thought about the door on the left, so she tried the knob and found it unlocked. The jagged, angry feeling from the other door told her it was a trap, or something worse.

The second room was too dark to see in, and she paused to listen for any sound to indicate where the man had gone, or how many others there were. It was sheer luck that she had been walking so carefully to avoid detection, or else she would have run face first into the wall that stood a few feet ahead of her. She felt around with her palm, gently skimming the cool and pebbly surface.

Another wall came up on her left, and the wall on the right ran in tandem with it for another six steps until it opened up. She curved right and continued until another segment of the wall met across from her to block her path. Allara sighed, knowing that if the room weren't so dark, it would confirm her suspicions that she was in the midst of some kind of maze. What possible enjoyment could her tormentors receive from this, when she was alone in the dark?

Allara gulped against her dry throat and continued her careful exploration of the maze, not risking her momentum to dwell. She closed her eyes and tried again for the feeling in her gut, fainter now and tired, as if it were an overused muscle. Her sense washed over her, more gently this time, and as if the floor had been illuminated, she found her way out. The effort was exhausting, so she stopped to catch her breath and realized there was yet another door for her to go through.

The third room, at least, had one large skylight to let in the soft, bluish glow of the moon. It pooled on the floor ahead of where she stood, outlining the vastness of the space. This room, too, seemed devoid of any furniture or signs of life. She took a few tentative steps into the room, until her foot caught in midair, and she careened forward. The makeshift weapon skittered out of her grip. On her hands and knees, she looked behind to find a hair-thin silver wire glinting mockingly in the moonlight.

Before she had the time to right herself, the whole room shook, and then the floor went out from under her. She fell a couple of feet, mercifully able to break her fall with her hands, though her wrists throbbed from the impact.

The ground below was hard-packed dirt, cool and dark. Disoriented as she was, she heard what sounded like celebration. Hoots, clapping, and laughter slowly came down into the pit she found herself in. She eased herself back toward the edge, for what little good that would do her.

Slowly, obscured faces popped up over the ridge of the pit. She couldn't keep the sneer off her face, although she knew it was unwise to antagonize these people. But her heart skipped a beat entirely when the last person came into view—curly auburn hair and amber eyes she'd recognize anywhere.

"I told you she'd make it to the last room." Taran smirked from above her.

CHAPTER FIVE
NYMM

Nymm had to remind herself to stop creeping about as she meandered through alleyways toward the gambling hall. She'd taken it upon herself to find out more about their current job, but she wasn't used to being so direct. It was forbidden to ask their fixer about the jobs they brokered, but there was no legislation against asking *any* fixer. Fixers tended to keep their cards close to their chests, so it was a long shot at best, but what good was being owed so many favors if they were never called upon?

Shae had agreed to a brief meeting during her fifteen-minute break. The fact that she'd agreed at all was mainly swayed by the friendship and whatever else they'd shared over the years. The Gilded Abyss, the main gambling hall of the Outer Circle, was brutal to those in its employment. Long hours, brusque patrons, and not enough gold to make any of it sting less. It meant something that Shae was willing to forgo the brief respite she'd earned to help assuage Nymm's fears.

The hall was crowded, and a line snaked out the left-hand side of the building, with patrons waiting their turn to bet away the meager coin they'd toiled for. The gambling hall in the Outer Circle made more money than the establishments in the Middle and Inner Circles combined. As such, it was the largest and nicest building in the area, only adding to the influx of the crowd. Four stories housed a variety of card tables, betting halls, and private rooms.

The line mattered little to Nymm. She wasn't using the front door anyway. Instead, she circled around the back, past the employee entrance below ground, to the alleyway where stairs led all the way to the roof in a spiraling matrix. They were in case of an emergency and protected with a barrier spell, but those had never stopped Nymm. Some of the older Fools and other *professionals* like them had crystals to dispel such wards. They were untraceable and appropriately high in cost, making them fairly rare. Auren carried one he coveted and had set into a ring, the thin brass band around a green stone that almost passed for a family heirloom—as if he came from the kind of family to have such a thing.

Nymm had no crystal; her blood was enough. It was what made being a Civarran so dangerous, and what made Valmaris so afraid—afraid enough to scatter and destroy almost every family line in Civara. It was no consolation for what she had suffered, but at least she had something they couldn't take away, though they tried.

The barrier fizzled against her skin as she passed through it, the sensation gone as quickly as it had started. She wound up the stairs without making a sound. Once she reached the fourth floor, she headed through the door to her left. Another barrier melted across her skin like a kiss.

Although she was deep in the employee wing, the clatter of dice and coins, shuffle of feet and chairs, and soft music drifted through the corridors. The maze of hallways was designed to ferry the small village of employees between halls and private rooms with ease. Nymm didn't bother navigating the labyrinthine paths; she simply turned right and followed the perimeter to a small balcony for smoke breaks.

She settled into the corner, brushing dark, wayward hairs behind her ears and taking in a breath of the stale city air. At this height, and being close enough to the shoreline, she could hear the lull of the ocean, imagine the way the moon and surrounding lanterns would sparkle against the peaks of the waves. It wasn't long until a rhythmic gait approached the balcony.

Uniforms were meant for just that: uniformity. But Shae wore hers like a choice, and like everything else, it suited her. She laughed lightly as she crossed the small balcony and tried to light a cigarette with a carnelian-powered lighter. "I don't know why I expected to get here first."

Nymm just shrugged as Shae fumbled with her lighter, starting and restarting it without a spark. When Nymm got fed up with waiting, she reached between them, fingers bathed in a warm orange glow.

"Thanks." Shae exhaled against the silhouette of the city, the high peaks of the Keep in the distance, the smog and clouds hanging close around them. The city was as alive as either of them, beating heart and all.

Nymm was glad, at least, that Shae hadn't seemed to change much in the years since they'd gotten to Oberon. Apart from possessing an otherworldly beauty that drew everyone in—including Nymm—she was honest to a fault. She'd never say anything she didn't mean, and Nymm hoped that meant she of all people would be able to help her get to the bottom of things.

"How's work been?"

Shae rolled her eyes and brushed a long strand of ruby hair behind her shoulder. "Really, Nymm? I haven't seen you in weeks, and that's the first thing you ask me?"

Nymm shrugged again.

"It's fine. As always. The pay is shit, but so is everything around here. It's enough to live on." She sighed. "So, you wanted to meet about your big job, right?"

Nymm chuckled. "I didn't say why I wanted to meet."

"No, but I can assume. It's all anyone can seem to talk about. And you never come to see me at work, so it must be important."

"Well?" Nymm tilted her head to the side. "What have you heard?"

Shae exhaled slower than necessary. Her gaze bounced around before returning to Nymm. "You know I can't say much, even if I knew anything at all. Which I don't."

"Come on, give yourself some credit."

Shae sighed and pouted a bit, although Nymm was sure she wasn't aware she was doing it. Nymm was used to the routine, the way her large, emerald eyes turned down in an argument until all you wanted to do was make her stop looking so sad.

Nymm continued, "You know I'd never ask anything of you that wasn't this important."

Shae's smile peeked through her frown. "I know." She picked at the cuticles bordering her short, stained nails. Her hands were the only things about her that weren't beautiful. They were honest, working hands. The day Nymm saw her with lacquered fingers and soft skin, she'd know the Shae she loved was gone. "But if word got out that I told you anything … with the way this job has been kept under wraps, they'd kick me out of my guild. Maybe worse." Nymm's mouth opened to interject, but Shae continued, "And it's dangerous for you too. There's a reason clients are kept private."

"I get it. But this whole thing…" She sighed. "It just doesn't feel right."

"I can't, Nymm, I'm sorry."

"I don't have much gold, but I—"

"Don't insult me. Keep your gold."

Nymm weighed her options. "I've never asked you for anything, and I never will again."

"That's not fair."

"Isn't it?" She raked a hand through her hair. "I'm not trying to hold it over you, but please. Consider this a favor repaid."

"After all these years, I always wondered what getting out would cost me."

"This isn't like that."

"Then what's it like? You saved my life just to endanger it all over again?"

"Shae, you're being dramatic."

Shae turned to her, sharp as a whip. "I'm being realistic, Nymm. This isn't how things are done, and you know that." She enunciated each harsh word. "If this is all you came to ask, then I think you should leave."

She returned the cigarette to her mouth as Nymm clenched her jaw. She wanted this to be easy. She had hoped that their history would have carried a bit more weight. Shae was something like family to her, going through what they had, but The Fools *were* her family now. And she'd do what was necessary to keep them all safe.

"I'm sorry, Shae, but I'm not asking."

Shae puffed out smoke just in time for it to coil around the dagger that landed at the base of her chin, the hazy air curling around it in tendrils before it dissipated.

Shae's laugh was bitter. "I've heard the rumors, you know. About The Fools and their desperation. I thought they might be exaggerating. I certainly didn't think you'd stoop so low."

"I don't care what they say about me."

"You don't care about much anymore, do you?" Nymm's silence was answer enough. "I can't blame you, really. After what we've seen… Nothing is sacred anymore, not even friendship."

Nymm crossed her heart behind her back, not wanting to give Shae any ammunition. It was bad enough that it had come to this, she didn't need to know how much she feared it.

Shae didn't meet her eyes for a moment—long enough to have beads of sweat gathering at the base of Nymm's neck. "Fine." A deep breath in. "This has been kept very confidential, even within my guild." Her body was stiff under the threat of the knife. "I don't know who the client is, but I can tell they're Inner Circle—nobility, maybe."

Nymm was unimpressed and held the knife steadier against her skin, enough to make her throat work with tension. "Well, with the payout, I would think so. But why do you say that?"

"I've seen a certain seal on some of the contracts, on more than one job."

"Describe the seal."

Shae paled. "I don't think that's a good idea. I mean, I don't think I was even supposed to see it. And giving it to you would definitely be breaking the code. I've already said too much."

"Just tell me what you saw, and I promise it won't come back on you."

"Saints, Nymm!" Her voice was a mastered perfection of hushed rage. Socially appropriate, but just as damning. "I wouldn't even know how to describe it. It's like nothing I've ever seen."

For all that they had been through, Nymm had never seen Shae this rankled. Not even when she was bleeding and fleeing her home in the middle of the night. Now, though, she heard the tremor in her voice beneath the indignation. And it wasn't fear of Nymm or the dagger sparkling in the light. Nymm knew her intuition was right, and the fear in Shae's eyes was for whatever was lurking at the edges of this job.

"I need to know. And then I'll leave."

Shae closed her eyes, in defeat or acceptance, and Nymm lowered the knife just enough to reach into her satchel and draw out a quill and parchment. Shae shakily grabbed each and began sketching out a design in broad, rough strokes. The sound of the tip scratching against the paper grated on Nymm's ears. Each stroke deepened the divide between them.

"Here." Shae held the sketch toward Nymm without looking in her direction, gaze fixed on her work boots and the stamped-out cigarettes that littered the ground. "We done?"

Nymm glanced at the drawing to make sure it was complete, then tucked it back into her bag before lowering the knife all the way. Shae's eyes didn't wander from the ground. Nymm, however, memorized this final glimpse of her. The dyed hair to fit in, the colored contacts to appear enchanting. Shae was beautiful, but that was her choice of weapon. Nymm chose daggers and secrets, while Shae chose to be desired. Neither erased where they came from, who they truly were. It tore at something in Nymm's heart to finally look away.

Shae dropped the nub of her cigarette to the ground and crushed it beneath her heel. "We've lost too much, you and I." She met Nymm's eyes for what Nymm knew would be the last time. "I hope this is worth losing each other too."

She turned back inside as Nymm raked in a deep breath. She shut her eyes and willed the tears forming not to fall. She'd had some naive hope that she wouldn't have to go that far—that against her better interest, Shae would break the code for her.

Worse still was the lingering certainty that sat heavy in her gut. Had Shae sensed it too? That although it would haunt her, although she'd be forsaking their saints and blood-lines, she would have used that dagger to make her point if necessary.

Nymm was in a foul mood, and her meeting with Shae had only exacerbated her feelings. It was starting to seem like all she spent her waking hours on was work, and her dreams were plagued with nightmares of her childhood. Masses of crowds being herded from one place to the next, suspicious eyes of guards in her village, forgotten toys and clothes that didn't fit into hastily packed bags... Tulvar had concocted a few potions for her to have a dreamless sleep, but in a way, that was worse. Waking from nothing on and on made her days bleed together into something bland and incomprehensible.

Nymm decided she needed to start her research with the books she already owned, then she'd try a bookseller or two. She didn't want to risk a library, which was funded by the crown, or the chance of anyone monitoring what she was reading. Things could come back on her and Shae, and she couldn't hurt Shae more than she already had. Luckily, however, between herself and Auren, they had amassed enough of a collection to serve as a decent starting point. Auren, especially, would follow a certain whim so strongly that he'd become an expert on the subject before abandoning it entirely.

She arrived home to find everyone present, and she was reminded of how desperately they needed the income and notoriety from this job. But that was all the more reason to be thorough. She couldn't let the allure blind her to any danger they might be in.

She climbed the stairs to her room, facing east, so she could watch the sun rise in the mornings. Her coat was folded into the trunk at the foot of her bed, and her bag hung across the back of the chair tucked into her desk, the only spot of mess in her entire room. Hidden among maps and half-finished books were past-due notices and eviction warnings. They only worsened her mood, since every active member of the Guild was currently home, not working, and not helping them to get out of the hole they'd found themselves in. Some days, Nymm felt like she was the only one keeping things together, but someone had to. And if all the responsibility lay with her, then so be it. She wouldn't—couldn't—lose another home. Having to give up everything she knew one more time would break her, she was certain.

She pushed the issue to the recesses of her mind and started rifling through the books stacked on her desk, tossing applicable tomes onto her small cot in the corner. After she'd gone through her own collection, she headed to Auren's room on the other end of the hall. Most of the rooms were empty, dust settling on the barren desks and unmade beds. Tulvar, Virgil, and the newer recruits shared two rooms below, leaving only Auren, Nymm, and Ilia on the top floor. Nymm and Ilia had shared a room for a few odd years, but with so much unused space, it seemed ridiculous not to spread out a bit. In truth, Nymm enjoyed the closeness sharing a room fostered, especially with the only other woman in the Guild. It was as close to sisterhood as she'd ever hope to have now.

Nymm knocked on Auren's door louder than she normally would to accommodate his poor hearing after a fist to the skull one too many times. He looked up toward her from where he sat at the edge of his bed, sewing the seam of a dark tunic that, by the looks of it, had already split a handful of times before. Crouched over the threadbare thing, Nymm felt a flash of sadness for him. He hadn't complained once, but she knew he needed the gold as badly as she did. He never treated himself to new things; if it didn't have a way to benefit the Guild or his work, Auren didn't buy it. He saved every coin he earned in a lockbox wedged underneath one of the floorboards. Nymm had always wondered what it was for, but never dared ask. It was the one mystery he held between the two of them, and Auren seemed to need to keep it to himself. Whether it was privacy, shame, or something else, Nymm had to respect it. He'd never pushed her to give more than she was willing, and despite her curiosity, she knew he deserved the same.

"Hey." Auren set down the tunic he'd been working on. "Anything good?"

Nymm shook her head. "Not sure, I'm still looking." She stepped out of the doorway. "Mind if I borrow a few books?"

Auren shrugged. "Be my guest."

Nymm settled down at the desk next to the bed, but Auren made no move to continue sewing.

"How's Shae?"

Nymm didn't have to even look at him to see the smirk he was giving her. It stung more than it usually would. "She's fine."

"That's all you're going to give me? You're maddening." He sat up. "You know, I always thought you two would—"

"Auren," she snapped, "leave it." She closed her eyes tightly, as if to keep in all her hurt.

"Fine, I won't pry. Sorry." He stretched back across the bed, resting his head in his hands. He began to hum under his breath, louder and louder as she tried to tune him out.

"Can you stop that?"

"*You* came into *my* room."

"Well, I'm trying to read."

Auren had nothing to say to that. He just kept humming until Nymm was fed up enough and chucked a nearby stick of charcoal at him. He caught it in midair, insufferably, and twirled it between his fingers. The clicking noise each time the charcoal skimmed over a knuckle made Nymm clench her teeth.

"Auren." It was a low warning.

"Nymm," he mocked, drawn out. "You're in a foul mood."

"So, you're trying to make it worse?"

"If that's what it'll take." Auren chuckled. "Talk to me." His voice was so earnest, she tried as best she could to let the anger redirect away from him and back into her own body where it belonged.

"I got a lead that I think will help. But it wasn't easy."

Auren hesitated. "You didn't...?"

"No." She exhaled. "Saints, never. But I don't think Shae will ever speak to me again."

"That bad?" She didn't answer. "I'm sorry, Nymm. I wish you wouldn't have done that for us."

"I didn't see another way to go about it."

"I trust you, in all things. So, please, remember that as I say this." She heard the bed creak as he shifted on it. "This is a job, same as any other. We just do what we're told, and we get paid when we're done with it."

Nymm sighed and set the book face down on the desk, so she wouldn't lose her progress. "You think I'm being paranoid?"

"It's not a bad thing to be cautious. But to lose Shae, for this? Do you not trust us to get this done?"

"No, I just..." At her hesitation, Auren stopped fiddling and sat up to face her. She continued, "Something about all of this feels wrong. It's like I can't stop looking over my shoulder, and it's driving me crazy." She ran a hand down the side of her face. "I feel like I'll never be able to relax. I just can't help but worry that…"

"Hey, that's not going to happen. Not here."

"You can't know that. What happened in Civara… No one could have foreseen that." Her voice turned quieter. "None of us were prepared."

"Whatever is bothering you, I trust it. But Civara? Nymm, that's impossible."

Nymm scoffed. "I need to know for certain. Shae was scared, Auren. Actually scared. I haven't seen her like that since that night."

Auren's swallow was audible. "Surely it can't be as bad as you're thinking."

"I think I'll always imagine the worst-case scenario. It's just who I am now."

Auren stood and walked over to the desk, putting his hand on her shoulder. "I'm sorry for what you've been through, and what you've given up, truly. But this isn't that. It's just a job, and we're all here to help. Maybe you can put those fears to rest, yeah?"

Nymm cleared her throat. "Yeah." She sniffed and straightened herself up. "Now, leave me alone and let me work."

Auren chuckled and returned to his sewing. They only had a few hours before the final bell, and then he was off for the initiations.

A pit settled in her gut. By all appearances, Nymm's mood had improved, and she did appreciate Auren's confidence. But her fears were not so easily assuaged, especially as she turned the page to find a seal that matched the one Shae had sketched at her demand—and her worries only grew tenfold. Shae had gotten it wrong. It wasn't a noble seal; it was much worse.

CHAPTER SIX
ALLARA

Taran reached down to help pull Allara from the pit. She hesitated, only slightly, but Taran's brow furrowed. She shook herself and took his hand. She couldn't make sense of the warring thoughts and emotions that coursed through her, but this was Taran. She tamped down the hurt she felt, the immediate need to reassure or comfort him. She hadn't wanted to hurt his feelings, but if he had known what she was about to go through... Had he already been through the same? She already knew this had something to do with The Fools, and her resentment bloomed at whatever stunt they'd just pulled on her.

Her feet scrambled against the dirt, and Taran pulled her up and over, bringing her to a stop in front of a small group. The man standing on his left she recognized immediately; besides his towering height almost reaching Taran's, the slicked-back curls and gloves stuck in her memory. Allara wished she'd gotten a better hit in at the docks.

Two younger people stood behind him and Taran, forcing looks of boredom. They didn't look like they belonged any more than she did. The third behind them was a man so tall, so wide, some animal part of Allara wanted to take a step back, to flee. The way his eyes traced her only added to the wariness, but her sense—though depleted—did not pick up any malice from him.

The last person to arrive was just entering the room as Allara was getting her bearings. She was slight, short, and barely made a sound as she came to a stop beside the man who'd attacked Allara. The way the energy shifted in the room, she could tell this woman was in charge, or at least important. Taran slid closer to Allara, his guilt radiating from him so ardently that she could practically feel it. When their eyes met, his conveyed enough without saying anything at all.

"Let me explain…"

"Not here."

Allara wasn't going to let him off so easily, but there was no reason to appear divided in front of these strangers. The man Taran had been standing next to—the one from the docks—arched a brow crossed with a shiny, pale scar.

"I'm sure you can guess what this is all about, and it's nothing personal. We had to make sure you'd be a good fit before we gave you a pin." His hazel eyes softened at the corners. "We all went through it."

"You two got much farther than the rest. Made for a good show." The larger man chuckled.

Allara took a beat before responding, "I haven't actually agreed to anything yet."

The first man turned a quizzical gaze on Taran, who fiddled with the charm on his bracelet. "Well, that's interesting. Your friend here seems to have spoken for you."

The woman beside him cut in, "We don't take anyone who's unwilling." Her tone was sharp enough for even Allara to feel chastised, and she wasn't the one who'd done anything wrong.

Allara's laugh was short. "I'm not sure you have the right person, then. I've no interest in a guild."

The woman's hard onyx stare turned on her, appraising. "Well, then, maybe that's not what we're offering. We just need to fill a job. Doesn't mean you need to wear the pin."

"And you'll have no problem cutting me loose after that?" Disbelief must have been written all over her face.

The man chuckled. "I don't know what you've heard about us, or the underworld, but it's a job, same as any other. Not a life sentence."

"I've heard plenty of worse things. And it's not like you all follow the law as it is," Allara shot back, just a bit more petulant than she needed to be because it was coming from him.

"We may be criminals, but we're not monsters. You'll do your job, get your cut, and we'll part ways. Simple as that."

"Where'd you get your skills?" The woman redirected their bickering.

"Odd jobs, I suppose."

"You don't have a trade?"

Allara's cheeks heated. "No."

The woman shrugged. "It's no matter to us. But your instincts are good."

Allara nodded, sensing that the woman was being genuine, and let some of the tension seep from her shoulders. "What's the job, then?"

The man frowned. "We can't reveal the details unless you've officially been hired."

"So, we're supposed to just go on your word?" Allara scoffed.

"You want the gold, right? Don't see how you have much of a choice. You accept first, or you walk."

"You need us."

He laughed. "We need *someone*. You're better than the rest

we've tried, but that doesn't mean we won't settle for another." He narrowed his eyes at her. "We don't need to bring anyone on who can't get along and follow orders."

"Will it hurt your feelings if I don't do what you tell me to?" Allara smiled sweetly.

"Enough," the woman barked, but it had no bite to it.

Allara wiped the smile from her face and turned toward the woman. "Can we have a moment?"

She just nodded.

Allara led Taran back into the hallway that she'd broken out of moments ago. Sweat still beaded on the base of her skull, and she was shaky from the comedown of the adrenaline.

"Allara, I—"

"Not now, Taran. Believe me, I'm not letting this go any time soon, but what's done is done. I need you to tell me what you know about these people."

"The man who approached me at the boxing club is the one I've spoken with the most, but he's not here. I've been talking to Auren while we waited for you to, uh … well anyway he seems alright."

"He's the jerk who attacked me, then?"

Taran let out a breath of frustration. "He's not a bad guy, so can you please keep your temper from spoiling this?"

"Oh, my *temper* has spoiled this? You let them kidnap me! I thought I was going to die, Taran! I thought Daia…"

Taran reached for her, and against her anger, her body's natural instinct was to melt into him. "I'm sorry, Allara. This is the way they do things. I had no say in the matter."

"But you've already told them I'd take the job?" His amber eyes turned down toward the floor, and it only angered her further. "We don't even know what we're getting into, what they want us to do. How could you just speak for me like that?"

"I did this for us, Allara." His hands tightened on her shoulders. "I couldn't risk them filling our spots with someone else. This kind of gold is life-changing. Think about it." He searched her expression, mouth turned down, then continued, "You'll never have to worry about getting Daia's medicine again."

Gods damn him, but he knew exactly how to win her over. "I know. But this is a guild, the underworld. I don't care what they say; we can't just walk away from this."

"Why are you so certain you'll want to leave?"

Her brows drew together. "Why would I want to be a criminal for the rest of my life?"

"What else are you going to do?" At the hurt that filled her eyes, he amended, "Shit, I didn't mean it like that, Allara." He sighed and dropped his hands. "I'm just afraid to lose this chance. But I can't do this without you. I won't. You have to see what an incredible opportunity this is."

She was hurt. Hurt at what he thought of her, which was really just what she thought of herself every day. She was hurt that he didn't trust her with this, to decide together. But really, it didn't grate on her as much as it should. She'd been the caretaker and decision-maker over she and Daia's lives for years now; some part of her felt unburdened to have a major decision like this taken out of her hands.

Her ego and pride swirled around in her thoughts, but all she could really afford to think of was her sister. With the resoluteness of that burden, she nodded. "Fine. Let's go back in."

Taran wrapped her in a hug, arms folding in at the center of her shoulders. When he spoke, it was muffled through her long, dark hair. "Thank you, Allara. I knew I could count on you. You won't regret this."

She sighed when he let her out of his hold, straightening

up and rounding her shoulders back. When they walked back into the room, only the two who seemed in charge remained.

"I take it we're back on track?" The man—Auren—looked between them. His smirk infuriated Allara, but she knew she'd have to keep a handle on herself for them to be able to work together. Now that there was no denying she was in this for good, she needed to approach it as professionally as she would any other task.

"Yes, we are. And we accept." She looked between the two of them. "So, what's the job?"

Auren laughed. "So serious. Congratulations are in order." He walked over and clapped Taran on the shoulder. When he got to Allara and saw the look in her eyes, he instead shook her hand. "It's not every day you land the job of the century."

The woman, who was still a mystery to Allara, sighed. "Auren's not big on the details, but lucky for you, that all comes from the fixer. Whatever is left up to us falls on me." She nodded, but made no move to shake either of their hands. "I'm Nymm. Come."

Falling in line, Allara wordlessly paraded behind Nymm, who only came up to about her shoulder. She seemed about her age, maybe, but so far was incredibly reserved and … normal? Allara wondered how she'd gotten into such a sordid line of work.

She led them through a door and down a new hallway, which opened to another room that seemed to be at the very front of the building. Several workstations lined the perimeter of the space, with alchemy kits, lockpicking gear, and blacksmithing tools littering different tables. Bookcases sheltered the far corner of the room, concealing that area from view.

The other members had retreated to this room. They sparred in the open space adjacent to the doorway. The weapons were dull, blunted things for training, but it still gave Allara pause. She'd only ever fought with her wits and surroundings, and failing those, she'd implemented her fists. She'd never even held a dagger before, blunted or not. She was overcome with the sick panic that, despite the reward, this all wasn't worth the risk. She wasn't cut out for this job or this life.

Her stride faltered, and she was already at the back of the group, so she fell behind. Taran glanced back at her, brows furrowed, and she tried to muster a smile. She knew the effort would be wasted on him when he'd see right through it, but it was as much for her benefit as his. She took a deep breath in, drawing her gaze away from the practice fight and toward the bookcases, which the rest of their group turned behind and out of view of the rest of the room.

A large oak desk occupied most of the alcove, littered with maps, notes, journals, and all the workings of what Allara assumed constituted the job. It shouldn't have surprised her, being that it was so complex, but she hadn't anticipated how much had already gone into it prior to their recruitment. It loosened a few of the knots tangling her stomach. They had a plan. They were working things out. Everything was already sorted for them.

She and Taran filed awkwardly along the front of the desk like chastised students as Nymm and Auren lined up along the other side.

"We've done a good bit of it before bringing you in," Auren started, "but don't worry, you'll get a good cut."

Allara narrowed her eyes ever so slightly. "Why is that?"

Auren sighed, as if inconvenienced by her question. "You're going to be doing the actual on-the-ground, day-of stuff. There's more risk." His hard stare met hers. "Does that answer suffice?"

With the back of her neck burning, Allara just nodded her

assent. Nymm, either used to Auren's manner or uncaring how they all got along, spread out a map without acknowledgment of the tension between the two. "This is the area we're working. We have a week to prepare you two."

Allara studied the map of the portion of the city. A large square bordered by shops and restaurants was displayed with sewer entrances, rooftop routes, guard stations—anything a criminal would want to know. "Wait—I know this area. You said a week? Are you saying this job is taking place during the festival?"

Nymm nodded. "Right at the heart of it."

"How can we accomplish anything in all that chaos?"

"We're professionals." She glanced between the two of them and amended, "And we'll get you up to our standards."

"In just a week?" Allara was starting to feel like the room had an echo, but she couldn't help her building incredulity.

"It's not a problem," Taran said with enough bite that Allara knew she should be keeping her mouth shut.

"Right." Auren sounded less than convinced. "So, we're each going to take care of different phases of the execution. And while we have something drafted, we need a day to see if you're going to fit the positions we've picked for you."

"What was all that, then? Felt like throwing us into a pit for fun?"

"For fun? No," he scoffed. "Well, maybe a bit. That was a competency test. You may not get yourselves killed, but that doesn't mean you can pull off what we need from each of you. So, we'll run some drills and make sure we're all up to the task, alright?"

"That's fair," Taran supplied before Allara could argue further. Internally, she seethed. She knew he had a reckless streak she had never possessed, but how could he be so flippant about both of their lives? Already, her temper was getting the better of her.

"Alright," she agreed. "So, what are we supposed to do?"

"I'm sure you've noticed the guards are doubling their efforts in pushing all the trash out to our circle?" They both nodded and Auren continued, "It seems there are to be talks between the Emissary and Valmaran officials about the precious gods." Allara didn't like his tone, and she was unable to keep the distaste off her face. Auren just chuckled. "There's someone at this meeting we're to *intercept*."

Allara's stomach roiled at his implied meaning. "Who?"

"That's need-to-know." Auren's tone left no room to argue. But there was some tension, from Nymm especially, that neither of the two wanted to acknowledge, or wanted she and Taran to pick up on. It made Allara uneasy that either they were keeping something about this job from them, or the whole Guild was in the dark. Neither bode well for them.

Nymm drew her finger along the tunnels that ran below the city. "Someone needs to be in the Web. We've lined up the rotation so that our guard will be in place when we need to hit the target."

Selfishly, Allara hoped it wouldn't be her. The Web—aptly named for the intricate and winding tunnels that spanned the entire capital—housed all of the jails, detention centers, and guard commands. It wasn't a place you'd want to find your-self in, on either side of the bars. She swallowed as Nymm continued, "We've already got a uniform and a route to follow. For now, Taran, that'll be you." She looked him up and down without an ounce of interest. "You've certainly got the build for it."

Taran laughed lightly. "Makes sense, I suppose."

Auren leaned in and pointed to a corridor of the Web that ran directly under the Keep. "You'll need to get yourself here."

"And do what?"

He shrugged. "Follow the route and keep from raising

suspicion. When it's time to grab our mark, you'll need to be ready, with a distraction or assistance, depending on how things go."

Auren drew his finger in toward the center of the map. "We need someone stationed here, near the ceremony, to keep an eye on things. Allara, we've given this to you. We're going to have our people moving about, and you need to keep an eye on the festival and the guard. If things get rowdy or something goes off, we need someone to be able to track everyone down if plans have to change." He met her eyes, and she was startled by the sincerity in them. "You'll need to have all of our backs. Are we right in assuming you'll be up to it?"

Allara nodded grimly. "Yes." In this, at least, there would be no arguing. With she and Taran's lives on the line, she had no choice but to rise to the occasion. And as little as she might think of The Fools, she didn't wish them to come to any harm either. "What about the two of you?"

"I'll be on watch via the rooftops, and Nymm will be on the mark in the Keep."

"In the Keep? Is that even possible? Doing what?"

"Let her worry about that." Allara opened her mouth to retort, but Auren held up a gloved hand. "If we attract any unwanted attention, it's best if we can each operate as independently as possible. If anyone ties us together, the whole operation is tanked."

Nymm stood back from the desk. "We'll give you the remaining details of your assignments separately. Taran is with Auren. Allara, you're with me."

With a passing glance toward Taran, she followed behind Nymm as she led her back into the center of the room and over to the only table with nothing on it. She leaned down and pulled out stacks and stacks of books, loose paper, and maps—more than Allara had seen gathered on the previous table.

"It might sound like you've been given the easiest task, but you can't know things have gone wrong if you don't know how they're supposed to go. You proved you have a decent level of observation, but you'll need to know all of this material front to back." She looked at Allara to make sure she was paying attention before continuing, "You need to know the guard routes, where they're stationed, and for how long. What vendors are nearest the square, what they sell, and who's running each booth. What the performances are, when they go on. You need to be aware of every detail."

"And what am I supposed to do if something isn't as described? With such a massive festival, I'm sure there will be changes—what then?"

"Use your wits," Nymm responded dryly. "I'm sure you can determine the difference. If it seems abnormal, then pay more attention. If something is drastically different, you need to check in with me or Auren, and we'll consider how to proceed."

"There's no way I'd be able to follow you into the Keep."

"We have a plan for that, and the rest of The Fools will be ready to get messages between us, so familiarize yourself with them. Faces, stature, and how they walk."

"How they *walk*? Truly?"

"If they're in a costume, you'll have to identify them some other way; their pins will be too recognizable to be worn openly."

Allara sighed. "You're right. It did sound a lot easier before you explained all this."

Nymm leaned in, voice lowered to only be heard between the two of them. "I assume you need the gold, like all of us do. So, I trust you'll do what it takes to get this done. If in any way I think you'll be a detriment to this operation, you'll be cut and replaced. So, do the job." Each word was enunciated with steely determination, but she leaned back and smiled as if they were having a genial conversation about the weather.

Allara knew then why this woman seemed to be in charge, why she very clearly was the one running things. Authority exuded from her every pore.

Sensing that her doubts were to be kept between the two of them, Allara simply nodded. She knew she couldn't speak a word of it to Taran, who would just accuse her of wanting to sabotage the whole thing. But now, for better or for worse, she was as bound by fate as the rest of them in this, and she'd see it to the end.

CHAPTER SEVEN
AUREN

In barely the blink of an eye, a week had gone by. Their new recruits were passable, mostly. Allara seemed to pick apart every word he spoke, looking for an angle to refute somehow. It was driving him to his wit's end, but luckily for them all, Nymm picked up on the tension a day in and took over most of her appraisal and training personally. Any time he saw her dark, nearly purple hair from down the hall or around a corner, he'd turn back the other way. It was getting so ridiculous that Nymm began to tease him incessantly about it. Allara just had a way about her that was unsettling to Auren. Of course they'd hire the one person immune to his charm. He supposed there had to be a first time for everything, after all.

She and Taran, however, did keep up with training much better than Auren had hoped for. Taran's job was mostly acting, and making sure he was good enough with a blade. And he seemed able enough to think on his feet should something almost certainly throw off their plans.

Allara was the surprise. A scrawny thing, with no trade or specialization to speak of, but she was more observant than she let on—almost unnaturally so. She picked up on how he favored his right leg a bit more when they sparred, and immediately recognized Nymm as the authority of the Guild. Whether that was due to her dislike of him, though, he wasn't certain.

So, all things considered, he felt cautiously optimistic about the job going off relatively smoothly. But ever since Nymm had come back from speaking with Shae, she'd been … off. Nothing obvious, but Auren knew her well enough to know her tells. Like the way she knocked twice before leaving the house, or crossed her fingers over her heart before saying something negative. Nymm had always been a bit superstitious—a hallmark of Civarran saints. If he thought the Avernan gods were complex enough, the saints put them to shame.

He'd tried asking Nymm what her research turned up, but she'd given only noncommittal responses. If it were anyone else, he'd be offended, but he knew Nymm was either waiting for certainty to reveal her findings, or she was cautious of speaking ill and jinxing their chances. He'd never understand how she balanced the saints from home and Averna's gods. He had asked, once, when curiosity no longer sated him.

"How can you believe in both?"

"Why can't I? When one lacks, the other helps."

"They contradict each other," Auren had scoffed. *"That's not how faith works. You can't believe in what suits you best."*

She'd just smiled. *"You don't think so?"*

Since then, he'd left her to her warring faiths, and in turn, he had more faith in her. He'd have to trust—no, he *did* trust that she wanted what was best for the Guild, and would do whatever was necessary to secure that future. So, while her doubts plagued his thoughts, he restrained himself from continuing to question her on it.

He lost himself in training, readying supplies, and looking over the last of the instructions they'd been given by the fixer. So far, the client had been incredibly piecemeal in providing instructions and revealing intel. It made things more difficult to plan out, but as it was the night before the festival now, he was sure they'd gotten everything they were going to get. It was up to them to see this through and walk away with more gold than any of them had ever dreamed of.

Being on the precipice of such a moment had made Auren introspective—so much so that when he'd usually be meditating and getting a good night's rest before a job, he instead headed down a familiar street in a familiar neighborhood and hopped a small wall into a tiny, well-tended garden, barely large enough to stand in. Since he'd last been here, new marigolds were in bloom, so lush and vibrant that they dominated the space of the old and established rosemary that filled the air with a fragrant smell.

In the waning light of the moon, the house looked smaller somehow. Or maybe it was that he'd grown enough so that it didn't loom over him as entirely as it had. It was just a place —a place he ached for down to his bones, but it was just four walls and a worn roof. The first thing he was going to do with all of his gold was buy a new roof, maybe add a few rooms as a second story. The possibilities were going to be endless for them—if he was allowed back in. The weight of that fact settled deep in his stomach as he approached the window and knocked five times in an offbeat pattern. He could be in another life, in another world, and he'd recognize the rhythm of those knocks in any of them. But would she?

Auren waited and waited as sweat beaded across his palms and upper lip. He'd almost thought to knock again when slowly, a shadowed silhouette approached the glass. A young, heart-shaped face came into view, with their mother's eyes, pale skin, and blonde hair that was wrapped up in a low bun. He'd always assumed her features came from the father they'd never met. She was a ray of moonlight, where Auren took entirely after their mother's warm, earthy tones. It made them look like strangers upon first glance. But it was always the eyes—eyes that now swirled with shock, concern, and something he couldn't quite place.

Her hand hesitated as she reached for the window latch.

"Please, Cyrie, it's important."

Mouth set in a hard line, she unlatched the window and pushed the rotted frame out toward him. He wedged his way through—it had been much easier years ago when he was smaller—and closed it tightly behind him.

Their room looked the same. His old bed sat forgotten in the far corner, piled instead with books and pages of notes. Cyrie's mind for numbers and formulas surpassed anyone Auren had ever met, even when she was only up to his elbows in primary schooling. In some ways, she still existed in his mind that way, young and full of laughter, constantly following him around. He knew it was a disservice to the woman she'd become in all those years since, but he'd always see the little girl he'd do anything to protect.

If only that was what she had wanted too.

He stuffed his hands in his pockets to avoid reaching for her. "You look good, kid. Still in school?"

"Yep." She'd backed away toward her side of the room, though it was all her room now. "Just one year left."

"Mom's still at the shop?"

At that, she rolled her eyes. "You know she is, Auren. She's seen your lackeys."

"I only asked them to keep an eye out for you both."

"Well, it's unnecessary. We don't need strangers following us around."

He tried to keep the frustration from his tone. This was a circuitous argument they'd had until the last three years, where they hadn't spoken at all. "They wouldn't be strangers if you'd let me check in. But you said you didn't want to see me, and I've respected that."

"You knew what I meant when I said that. I don't need you poking around; I can take care of myself. We both can."

"Do you really expect me to live in the same city, the same circle, and just hope you're alright? That you're alive? We're family, Cyrie. We look out for each other."

"You can barely look out for yourself," she scoffed.

"You sound just like our mother. Are these your words, or hers?"

"As if I don't have a mind of my own? I remember how things used to be."

Auren sighed and ran a shaky hand through his hair. "It's been a long time. I'm not that kid anymore."

She tilted her head, assessing. "Aren't you? I've heard about The Fools. Everyone has."

"Exaggerations."

"You're criminals, aren't you? That's all I need to know."

Her words struck deep, and Auren tried not to let the conversation get away from him. He'd always been more successful with his fists than his words. "Whatever you think we get up to, it's not all that bad. You know this city is corrupt; not all laws are meant to be followed."

"If that's what you need to believe, then I won't argue it. But the rest of us survive and make a living within the law." She paused. "Without hurting anyone."

"We've been over all of this before; I don't expect you to see things my way. But I need you to hear me out. We've got something that's going to change things. For all of us."

"Another scheme? We don't want your gold, Auren. We get by just fine between the two of us."

"You're not listening, Cyr. I'm on the brink of earning us

enough gold to move out of here. Inner Circle, Mancia, anywhere."

Cyrie scoffed. "Whoever told you that was lying to you."

"This is real, and it's big. Once it's done, we'll be set for life."

Cyrie sat down on the edge of her bed. She was nearly the same size as it, no room to toss and turn or curl up in the colder months. "Would you be done after this?" He hesitated, only for a moment, and her face fell. "When is it enough, Auren? When you're in jail? Dead?"

"I just wanted to come home. All these years, that's all I've wanted. But now, the Guild? They're family too."

"What if we asked you to come home? If we truly wanted to start over someplace new?"

"Then my choice would be made. You, always. But until then, please don't ask me to choose."

"You really care about them that much?"

"Yes."

She sat for a moment, as if thinking. Something he'd always admired about her was the way she truly listened. So, he waited, because he knew each word had sunk in, that no breath was wasted.

"Fine." A soft smile broke through her lips. "Tell me about all of your adventures, then. I miss your stories."

Auren sat on the floor in front of her as she sat cross-legged on her bed and nodded along to his favorite escapades. He had a knack for telling tales, and Cyrie laughed or gasped whenever it was appropriate. She had always been his favorite audience. The years that had wedged them apart melted away story by story until a little girl sat in front of him, who just reached to his elbows and followed around wherever he went.

They talked so long through the night that the sun rose, banishing the moon to welcome the longest day of the year.

With the sun already out in the early hours, it was hard for Auren to tell how much time he had left, but he knew he needed to be going. Nymm would want to go over everything one last time, and she'd be cross to see he wasn't home, hadn't slept. She'd worry, as she worried about everything else, that he wouldn't be at his best.

He slowly stood, knees protesting at how long they'd been locked in his position on the floor. "I'd best be going."

Cyrie shook her head as if waking from a trance. "Is it time already?" Then her eyes widened. "Oh, Gods, it's the festival! Today's the day?"

Auren nodded. "Just one more day."

She shot up and wrapped her arms around his middle. His chin rested on the top of her golden head. "Come back after, okay? To tell me how it went?"

"Of course. But promise me you'll stay home."

"And miss the festival? Why?"

"I don't want to worry about you being out there if something were to go wrong. Can you just trust me on this?"

She hugged him tighter. "Yes." Her next words came out muffled from how tightly she was pressed against his chest. "I'm sorry, Auren, for all the time I've wasted. I know your heart."

He placed a kiss on the crown of her head. "There's nothing to be sorry for. Love you, kid."

"Love you too." They separated, and he squeezed her shoulders, getting one last look at her, how she'd changed over the years. Seeing her from afar was so different. Now he soaked in the freckles that had darkened with the season's sun, the shadows under her eyes. It was still her, and she'd forgiven him. "See you tomorrow."

He went back out the way he came, the window creaking with his weight. The sun was warm across his shoulders as he crept through the garden, the subdued nighttime blooms now reaching up to meet the sun's rays.

The warehouse was quiet when he returned, and he almost wondered if everyone was still asleep before Ilia popped her head up from behind the kitchen counter.

"Oh, Auren, good morning. I didn't even hear you come in." She was digging through a stack of pans, her iron prosthetic peeking out from her dark cotton pants, catching the stray sunbeams.

"Just clearing my head. Need help with breakfast?"

She smiled up at him. "Sure, thanks." She nodded to the small table behind them. "Scramble some eggs for me?"

He washed his hands in ice-cold water, then mixed the eggs briskly with a fork.

Ilia's mess of dark curls moved along his periphery. "Today feels strange."

Auren laughed. "Today has barely started."

"Well, you know. With the job, it seems like we're on the brink of something. I just hope it all goes well."

"When has one of Nymm's plans ever gone awry?"

Ilia laughed in that birdlike way of hers. "Right. Well, think of all the interesting ingredients we'll be able to buy."

"You know, I've read about a technique from the Republic Isles where they ferment beans, and—"

Nymm came down the steps so quickly and silently that Auren almost jumped. "Good, you're up. I want to go over everything one last time before we brief the others."

Auren passed over the egg mixture to Ilia. The sound of it sizzling in the pan followed him as he passed into the living room, where the furniture had been cleared to the perimeter to make space for a makeshift command center. Things were starting to feel like normal again. It had been too long since they'd had a job briefing; too many of their recent jobs hadn't needed one.

Auren leaned over the table littered with maps, manifests, transcripts, and all the instructions they had been provided with.

Nymm gave him a long look, then in a hushed tone, she said, "I take it you won't be distracted today?"

The back of Auren's neck heated. Foolish of him to think he'd be able to get anything past Nymm. "It wasn't like that. I, uh, went to see my sister."

"Oh." Nymm smiled. "That's good."

"Yeah, it was." Auren nodded down at the map spread across the table between them. "You think we're ready?"

"As ready as we can be."

"Well, that's reassuring." Auren chuckled. "What's got you so rankled?"

Nymm paused for a while before answering. "I just have an off feeling."

"We've gone over everything—multiple times. Everyone has been training. What more can we do?"

"Just be ready, that's all."

"Are you ever going to tell me what you found out after you spoke to Shae?"

Nymm let out a quick breath of frustration. "Her lead didn't pan out. I don't know if she misdirected me or was wrong, but it was nothing."

"Then relax. Truly, we have a good team. By the time the sun sets again, we'll be the richest people in the Outer Circle."

Nymm scoffed. "That's not saying much. But you're right, we need to get this done and get things back on track."

"What do you mean?"

Nymm's brows crinkled in confusion. "With the Guild, of course. We can get things back to how they used to be around here."

Auren shifted on his feet, weighing his options. They

were on the brink of something so life-changing, but it might not be in the ways she was expecting. He'd thought to keep it to himself until it was necessary, but at her excitement, the pressure in his chest grew so strong that he had to say something. "About the Guild, Nymm, I—"

"Can we talk later?" She met his eyes. "I'm sorry, it's just, my mind is in a hundred different places. I promise if we talk later, you'll have my full attention."

The anxieties tangling up inside Auren didn't abate, but he still responded, "Yeah, of course." By the time the job was done and the gold was in their hands, he might lose his nerve, but that would be a problem for future him.

Nymm gathered up a few documents. "You alright to start the briefing after breakfast?"

Auren met her eyes and nodded, swallowing down the lump that had formed in his throat. He didn't like to start a job with things left unsaid; it clouded the air and his thoughts. And this final part of the job had the most moving pieces of any they'd taken on, separating across the Circles to get it done. They were strapped for help, even with the new recruits, and were working against a large crowd and tight security.

But Auren had faith in Nymm, even if it was the only semblance of faith he held. It had served him well enough all these years—more than any prayer to the gods that had passed through his lips.

Now, everything he wanted was within his grasp, and it was up to him to secure it. His family would take him back, and the Guild would be alright. Nymm would be okay without him; once The Fools were back on top, she'd hardly have the time to spare a thought for him. And he'd visit her, of course. She was like a sister to him, and even though she'd probably say the opposite, he knew she felt the same.

All that was between him and everything he wanted was this one last job.

CHAPTER EIGHT
ALLARA

Sweat was starting to bead up where Allara's skin met the mask. It was a gaudy, gold-painted thing that Nymm had procured for her to better blend in. Most revelers wore masks of Thiane or other gods to celebrate the festival, and at first, Allara preferred the anonymity of hiding her face. But as the sun beamed down onto the courtyard and her anxieties knotted up her stomach, she lamented the heat of the metal.

She'd only been at her station for the better part of one bell. The briefing in the morning had done nothing to calm her nerves, although the repetition bolstered her confidence slightly. Not only did she know her own part in all this completely, she knew where everyone else would be down to the letter. She'd drilled with Nymm on all the schedules of the day, who was invited, the vendors down each alley—there was no detail deemed unimportant. Allara had spent the previous night staring at the ceiling, imagining all the ways in which things could go wrong, and how she'd be the cause of it.

But Taran and the others were counting on her. Daia was

counting on her. So, she wandered through the row of stalls selling flags and banners, confections, jewelry, and all manner of overpriced goods. As soon as the sun set the following day, the streets would be littered with trinkets and trash left behind by tourists who had spent their purses and gone back to their normal lives. Some of the trash could be scavenged for a bit of gold, but most of it was worthless. Made for nothing and sold at ten times the cost, all it was good for was to litter the streets and leave something for the critters to pick at.

As Allara pretended to browse the stalls, she kept an eye on the guards along each intersection of alleys and stores. She was getting nearer to the main courtyard, where the stage was set up for the performances, sitting just outside the walls of the Keep. Despite her anxieties and preoccupations, she felt nostalgic among the sunny colors, sweet smells, and cacophony of sounds that entrenched the area. She could almost taste the candy floss she and her sister had shared one year—the year their father was so generous with his gold that anything they even glanced at was purchased for them.

Allara, being nearly seven, had delighted in being spoiled by her father. But the crease between their mother's brows grew deeper and deeper with each coin given away, until she pulled him aside while Allara and Daia were preoccupied with a puppeteer. Allara didn't hear what was said, but the harsh whisper of her mother's voice was unmistakable, as was the rigidity in her father's shoulders as he stalked away.

Allara didn't see him for the rest of the festival, or for the next two weeks … until one night, he came home reeking of pipe smoke and crashed through the cabinets and drawers, waking the whole family up. Her parents fought, like always, and her father stormed out with an armful of her mother's things. The guard found him a night later, and again and again after that. He saw the bars of a cell and the flush of cards more than his own daughters, his own wife.

Allara still loved the festival, but since that year, a bit of the wonder had been stripped away. Then, when Daia fell sick, it was just another opportunity for a bit of gold. Now, at least, there was more than a bit at stake, and Allara shook herself from her thoughts as she entered the main courtyard.

Banners and ribbons in mustard and ruby crossed above everyone's heads, woven through with lanterns and crystals that glowed despite the sun still raging high above them. A full band was stationed off to the right-hand side, playing something upbeat enough that children and young couples swirled around, laughing and clapping to the rhythm.

The main stage was dead center, the pointed peaks of the Keep in the distance serving as a grandiose background. It was between performances, but Allara knew the fire dancers were set to perform next. She mentally compared the various schedules with the day's events. Taran should be about a third of the way through his faux rotation down in the Web, and Nymm should have made it into the Keep by now. There was no way to know if they'd all been successful until they were due to meet back at the warehouse, or—gods forbid— one of the runners came to find her if things really went to shit.

Sixteen guards were scattered just across her field of vision, and she knew there were scores more. She still worried whether they'd be able to pull this off during the most heavily guarded day of the year. Nymm she trusted to be capable of most anything; Auren and Taran ... not so much.

Slowly, dancers in ornate silks with chains dripping from their wrists, waists, and ankles took to the stage. The metal was adorned with tiny little beads that twinkled gently as they swayed. The sound of the crowd and crush of people grew heavier as they all drew in to watch the spectacle. A flurry of activity behind the stage—more dancers, perhaps? She went over everything again in her head. Six dancers were set to perform, with another four joining for the finale. Only five were onstage currently.

Allara frowned and scanned the area surrounding the stage for the wayward dancer. It seemed silly to be concerned about such a thing, but Nymm had said trouble could come from anywhere. A commotion came from the left-hand side of the stage. A dancer was hastily tying the ribbons around her waist, a sparkling flurry of urgency as she joined the remaining dancers onstage. Each one had a different crystal projecting a unique colored flame, all bright and captivating as they swirled in unison to the music of the band. It was mesmerizing—so mesmerizing that Allara had to redirect her focus away from the main stage.

She heard the cooing and applause of the crowd for what she was sure were spectacular moves from the dancers. But instead, her gaze stuck on two people under the arch of an alleyway off the square. They huddled in its shadow, heads bowed and shoulders drawn in toward an invisible pull. They talked for another few moments until one drew away, farther into the shadows and toward gods knew where. The remaining figure—tall, dressed in all black—looked back and forth before walking toward the corner of the stage they were closest to. A knife glittered within their left hand as they passed into the heavy beams of the sun.

There was a purposefulness to their stride that set Allara's own feet in motion, following along their path like a moth drawn to flame. She kept a respectable distance, bobbing and weaving through the throngs of people so as not to lose her target. But what would she do once they stopped? The better question was what they had planned, why they were armed. She'd acted on pure instinct in trailing them, but adrenaline alone wasn't enough to carry her for anything else. If they were up to something, what could she really do? Call the guard? Find a Fool? She'd been sparring with Nymm for the past week, and she knew she'd improved, but a week was hardly enough to feel prepared for an altercation. If the gods were on her side, it wouldn't come to one at all.

They reached the edge of the stage where the remaining dancers and other performers stood, stretching or adjusting their costumes to sit perfectly. But once they reached a certain distance, they stopped, turning to look at the roof surrounding the area. Then, they turned to one of the remaining dancers set to join in the finale and bent over, mouth hovering near her ear. She nodded along as their lips moved so rapidly, Allara couldn't even hope to make out any of the words that passed through them. The dancer met their eyes and moved back toward the rest of the performers, glancing in the same direction toward the roof. There were only a handful of guards—and Auren—that were supposed to be up on the roofs. What could be drawing their attention? What was so important that it had to be spoken now, in the midst of the performance?

A gnawing in Allara's gut told her not to leave it, that it wasn't nothing. That bizarre feeling that came from her sense was that this person had ill intent. The malice beaming from them tangled in her gut as if the knife had already embedded itself in her flesh. If anything, checking in and being paranoid was her entire portion of the job. She knew where the Fools would be; Nymm had stationed one on each end of the court-yard, north and south, so that when it was time to move, they could all tighten in around the target like a knot being tied on a rope.

She was closer to the north, so she set off in that direc-tion, the cheers of the crowd fading as she gained distance, their fervor matching her calculations that the remaining dancers had taken to the stage for the finale. In another world, she'd be laughing and enjoying the spectacle too. Maybe once she had all the gold she'd been promised, she and Daia could enjoy airy candy floss and watch the performances from a private tent.

The crowd was so thick that she struggled to push through the revelers. Shining masks in gold and silver stared blankly at her, unnerving in their apparent apathy. The music, the shrieks from children, the shouting from the vendors promoting their wares—it was all so much to block out. But Allara knew where to go. Even if her mind couldn't make sense of things, her body did the work for her. Through the maze of stalls, she ended up down an alley, quieter than the center of the festival, but no less packed.

A tavern was situated in the center, barrels and crates making up temporary tables for the patrons that spilled out onto the narrow street. Lights crossed above the area, making it look almost romantic. Normally, beggars would be dripping from every corner, trash decorating the cobblestones. Allara scanned the crowd for Virgil. He was the last person she wanted to go to, but time wasn't on her side, and he was situated the closest to where she had been. Mean, and always looking at her too long, too closely; in her week of knowing him, she'd tried to never speak with him alone.

But it was a job, and she assumed he wouldn't be a liability. Luckily for her, he was a beast of a man, as tall as he was wide, and though Allara wasn't sure what mask he'd donned, she had no trouble seeking him out among the revelers. He was at a table with two other men whose masks were scattered on the table, face up. They were singing some bawdy tavern song, ruddy-cheeked and sloshing about wooden cups of ale.

Allara rolled her eyes internally. Virgil, at least, had the sense to keep on his own mask. She walked up to their table, ignoring the way the other two men drank her in. She gave him a moment to register that she was standing there, that it was her, but he made no move to acknowledge her presence.

"Thomaz," she snapped. Of course she'd had to memorize all of their ridiculous code names. "Time to go."

"Whyyyyyy?" he whined, sounding like a child rather than the wagon of a man he was. Allara studied him. He swayed gently in his seat, and had unbuttoned his lilac shirt almost to the navel. Was his act that good, or had he really gotten drunk in the middle of the biggest job in history?

"We're just getting started, love. Come join us," one of his table companions crooned.

Allara rolled her eyes. "Sorry, we're expected elsewhere." But her tone sounded anything but contrite. "Thomaz," she tried again. "Please."

"Okay, okay," Virgil slurred, moving to stand and almost immediately falling back onto the crate, which groaned under his weight. The whole table burst into raucous laughter, and Allara let a breath out slowly through her nose. There would be time to rip into him later, but for the moment, she needed to leash her temper and get him away so she could decide what to do. Although, in his state, she wouldn't expect him to be able to make it to Auren or Nymm with a message anyway.

"Up you go." She roused him, bearing his weight with her shoulder lodged under his arm. He was unbelievably heavy, and with the way his body sagged carelessly, it only made his weight that much more pressing. She hobbled him down the rest of the alley and around the corner, where they met a dead end piled with trash and boxes of supplies for the tavern. Allara eased Virgil down onto one of the boxes, massaging her aching shoulder. "What's the matter with you?!"

Virgil fumbled with the face of his mask, a black-and-white harlequin that looked much more jovial than she'd ever seen him. She helped his clumsy fingers with the straps. His face was slick with sweat, but his cheeks were a grayish tint against his normally golden skin. Allara leaned in. "Are you feeling alright?"

"Don't know," he slurred. As Allara met his eyes, she noticed his pupils were the smallest pinpricks, barely distinguishable in the sea of umber of his irises.

Allara leaned back. "How much did you drink?"

He thought for a long moment—so long that Allara thought maybe he hadn't heard her.

"Just an ale, to blend in. Not sure I even finished it."

A man his size should hold well more than *maybe* one ale. "You ordered at the bar?"

"Yeah, I..." He started to pant, as if he'd been overworked. "I..."

"Oh, Gods." It was obvious then. The color of his skin, his disorientation... He'd clearly been drugged—poisoned, maybe. Allara went to open the satchel she'd been outfitted with, then instead reached for his, strapped against his thigh. Allara might need her own supplies for herself, but as she rifled through the vials and pouches Tulvar had put together, it was clear she had no idea what she was working with.

Nymm, or Auren maybe, might know what kind of substance he'd been given, what he needed. But Allara didn't have the time for that; she still had to find another Fool to relay a message. So, she began pulling out the various antidotes and pouring them down Virgil's throat against his sputtering and coughing. She hoped none of them had any adverse effects, and that one of them would work.

Warring with herself for a moment, she set down his satchel and checked his pulse, faint and a bit quick, but still there. Nausea surged in her gut at the thought of leaving him so ill and disoriented in some alley, but they'd all have bigger problems if she didn't track down someone else. The fact that someone had gotten to Virgil sent a bolt of fear through Allara's heart—they could've gotten to anyone else too. She sent a prayer to the gods that everyone else was alright, and left Virgil in the back of the alley. Hopefully, any wayward pickpocket or other thief would think him a drunk or beggar and leave him be.

Her feet pounded against the cobblestones as she tore through busy, decorated alleyways toward one of the younger recruits in the south position. Ivan, his name was, but past the who's who for the job, she hadn't really gotten to know the Fools. What would be the need, she'd told herself, if she was out after this?

But she wasn't worried about after the job anymore; she was worried about right here and now: someone was trying to pick them all off. She knew to trust her gut; it had never been wrong before. Even when it had gotten her into trouble. Now, though, it might be the only thing to save their lives.

She just needed to find someone and tell them the job had been compromised, and pray to the gods that they trusted her enough to believe her. It'd be up to Nymm to decide how they should proceed—if they should proceed at all. But at least she'd have done her part, and then the decision would be out of her hands. But as she neared the stall Ivan was supposed to be stationed by, she found it empty. A man sold ribbon wands in the signature colors of Oberon and Averna, woven and braided into intricate patterns that danced on the wind when waved. A small line had formed at the front of the booth, and another was sandwiched right up against its side.

Ivan should have been here, somewhere. Allara made a quick circle of the immediate area to see if he'd just moved to a different position. But there was no sign of him. He was of average height and build, a bit on the skinnier side, like the rest of them. And young—too young for this life, Allara thought, but maybe it wasn't really her place to judge. As she completed her round and made it back to the booth, something sparkling on the ground caught her eye.

A Fools pin sat between two cobblestones, the bottom of it chipped off. As Allara leaned down to retrieve it, she realized the shine hadn't come from the cheap metal of the pin, but instead the blood that coated it. She recoiled like the thing had burned her. So, Ivan was gone too. The sick truth settled into Allara's gut that none of this had been a coincidence. Someone was after them, trying to sabotage them, or worse. And so far, it was working. Had the person she'd seen in the square been looking for her?

Screw the whole damn job and the gold. Allara headed for the last place she'd ever want to be in Oberon. She needed to get Taran and get away while they still had the chance.

CHAPTER NINE
NYMM

It had been deceptively easy to break into the Keep—what should have been the most secure building in all of Oberon, maybe even all of Averna. Nymm knew she was good, but the saints must really have been perched on her shoulder for how well things had gone thus far. She was slightly unnerved by how few guards she'd come across. All of the information she'd been given had indicated a heavier presence, but perhaps they'd been drawn elsewhere because of the festival. If they'd all gone farther into the Keep for the summit, then that would make her job much more difficult.

She'd gotten past the gate by scaling the wall, climbing down one of the guard turrets, and ending up inside the Keep's borders. Within the towering stone, it was like a village itself: a small farm, shops, blacksmiths, all manner of amenities were situated within walking distance from the main Hold. The Hold was a gargantuan thing, towering peaks forming an intricate profile like that of a sculpture. This was the closest she'd ever been, and would ever be again, but she had no time to take any of it in.

The corridor she snuck into bustled with urgency. A thick,

herbal scent clung to each stone, as if the area had been cleansed recently. The polished marble beneath her feet reflected the rainbow of sconces that lined her path. Though the sun would not take its leave for many hours yet, each lantern was lit with the largest crystals Nymm had ever seen —each surrounded by ornate and delicate glass. It was a gross display of magic, the power of which could light the hearths of several neighborhoods within the Outer Circle.

As it was a servants' corridor, she didn't have to worry about the presence of guards except at the exits and entrances, the latter of which she had circumvented by entering through the skylight on the roof. Such pretty displays made for weak points in safety, and Nymm was glad for the Inner Circle's frivolity.

What Nymm hadn't expected was the disgust that settled into the pit of her stomach. She knew the Hold would be ornate—extravagant, even. But the excess of it was appalling. Gold, sapphires, diamonds, all shrines to Valmaris. This, while her home was buried in the dirt, while a third of the citizens in the Outer Circle didn't have a place to call home. She could pry a single stone from the wallpaper, banister, any of the surfaces within arm's reach, and pay off the mortgage for the warehouse and buy a second one.

But she wasn't here for that, and didn't want to risk the displeasure of the saints by stealing. Even if it felt more like justice than a crime. Instead, she continued on her careful route up toward the meeting chamber where they expected their target to be, barely making a sound. She could hear the distant celebration of the festival below; music, laughter, and shouting melded into a synergism of noise. But the Hold itself was quiet. If she hadn't received verified documents of the meeting taking place, she would have assumed there was no one inside at all.

As she passed through the halls, she glanced at the ceaseless number of paintings that adorned the walls—landscapes, studies of buildings, even some portraits, familiar and unfamiliar to her. She could recognize the Emissary well enough, due to her likeness stamped onto all of their gold, but the woman beside her she had never seen before. A sister? A lover? Nymm had never heard of the Emissary having either, but she hadn't heard much about the Emissary at all. Yet she recognized the warmth between the two. The Emissary's coloring like the sun contrasted so beautifully with the woman next to her, moody and soft like the moon. Nymm looked closer at her then, the crook of her nose and the shape of her lips. So familiar, so like home.

But Nymm didn't have time to ponder the warring thoughts that creased her brow as she followed her rigid path. It wasn't until she reached the end of that portion of the servants' corridor that she ran into her first obstacle—an expected obstacle, but a problem, nonetheless. She'd been given false trade permits to be a maid servant, deemed an impressive counterfeit by Allara, that she'd tucked into the skirts of her uniform—a ridiculous thing she'd had to truss up and bundle about herself in order to climb rooftops and walls just to enter the Keep undetected. Now it swished around her ankles with her brisk pace, spinning around her as she stopped abruptly to face the guard who stood at the frame of the door out into the main chambers, tall and ruddy-faced. She did her best to smile sheepishly at him as she passed over her papers into his waiting hand. He looked back and forth between the two with an ever-increasing frown, until he grunted and returned the documents, nodding that she might pass.

Nymm didn't waste time on a formality, ushering herself into the adjoining rooms. Based on the blueprints they'd been given, this wing of the Hold was organized in a large semicircle, with the meeting due to take place at the opposite end. The rooms that lay between were smaller meeting chambers, offices, and the smaller of the Hold's libraries.

This wing was such a stark contrast, alive with flurried activity and noise. Servants in similar dress to her own bustled about with linens, livery, and decorations. Mages convened in the main atrium to light the lanterns that adorned the crown molding. The domed ceiling was filled with projections of dozens of butterflies flying across the floral fresco. Nymm hadn't seen illusion magic in years—not since home—and her chest cracked with the nostalgia of it. Her oldest brother, Li, had been particularly fond of illusions, putting on shows for all of their siblings after evening meals. He'd weave tales with princesses and dragons, knights fighting demons... Any story that was possible, he'd bring to life.

Here, magic was just used to impress the dignitaries, and to give the nobles something to gossip about. But magic could be—no, it *was* more than that. And to see it used so lifelessly made Nymm's blood surge hot in her veins. She pushed those feelings to the recesses of her mind.

She hurried through the halls, but wasn't spared a glance; everyone seemed to be hurrying about for something. The air hummed with the undercurrent of importance. As she reached the antechamber to the meeting room, she steeled herself. Nerves didn't usually get the better of her, but the worries from the past two weeks still loomed in the shadows of her mind. She wished things were different—that they could learn who had hired them, that they wouldn't have needed this saints' cursed job at all. But things were what they were, and she needed to do the job.

At the edge of the atrium, a gold-and-velvet bench sat under a tall arched window. Sunbeams streaked across Nymm's thighs as she used the bench for leverage and swung up to the top of the frame. From there, it was barely wide enough to stand, but the skylight above was in arm's reach—mostly—and she latched onto the edge of it, fingers straining with the effort.

She'd been relatively silent so far, but unlatching the pane of the skylight proved to be a challenge. It creaked terribly as she tried with her left hand to pop it out enough so that she could squeeze through. It was rusted and heavy, but with the surge of adrenaline from hearing the clack of boots growing closer and closer from down the hall, she pushed it open and sprung herself through—just in time for a guard to do a roundabout of the atrium before continuing on their route.

Nymm leaned on the glass below her, catching her breath and taking in the view. It was higher up than she'd ever been —higher than she could have gotten on any normal rooftop. The streets below looked so small, so narrow, but she could just make out the rainbow of festival decorations: banners and lanterns that crossed the city in a chaotic pattern. The crowds looked as big as grains of rice; even guards on rooftops only a handful of stories below looked to be no bigger than the width of her fingers.

She could admit how beautiful the city looked. Although, she supposed anything would be beautiful from this high up. Since time was not on her side, she straightened up and walked carefully to the perimeter of the atrium's roof. The domed surface provided little purchase for her boots, but she managed it in small, even steps. From there, the meeting room was rectangular, lined with skylights and floor-to-ceiling windows. Nymm peered into one of the glass panes.

Servants were bustling about below, setting up the final touches before the Emissary and invited dignitaries arrived. Thirteen plush armchairs were set in a circle toward the center of the room, with individual tables and footrests bordering each. A long banquet table stretched across the back half of the room, littered with confectioneries and delicacies the likes of which Nymm hadn't ever seen before. Auren would be so jealous when she described the feast that lay below.

These skylights didn't open—they were much too high above the floor—so Nymm brought out her knife. Auren had shown her how to sharpen it to a lethal point, thin and delicate as a blade of grass. She concentrated briefly, and flame erupted from her palm, heating the metal until it was a bright red as if it had been left in a forge. She carefully cut a small corner into the window pane, attaching a ball of resin to the back so she could keep it from crashing down to the floor below. She used another ball of resin to affix a palm-sized obsidian crystal onto the inside of the glass. The opening she'd made was so small that she had to feed the gem through sideways. She secured it to the interior side of the glass and sat back, resting her hand over it from the outside.

Deep down, she had known this was why they'd been hired for the job. Why she'd tried so hard to find the client, even sacrificing her relationship with Shae. She'd brushed off Auren's questions, lied—and he'd believed her so easily. But Auren had never known what their client somehow knew: that Nymm was a mage. It was something she'd need to tackle after the job, finding the client's identity and how they knew that about her. Or if anyone else knew too.

Only a mage could harness sound inside a crystal, especially for long enough to record an entire meeting. As far as Auren and everyone else knew, she just had to watch the meeting and grab the target after. But when she had opened her book to the seal Shae described, she saw a little note stuck in the binding of the pages, with instructions only for her, written in Civarran symbols—that she'd have to use her magic to record the meeting's words before the target was taken, or the whole job would be forfeit.

Nymm had wanted to back out, but how could she have explained why?

She waited as dignitaries slowly filed in, flanked by advisers, guards, and personal servants. They all wore the severe dress of Valmaris—sharp angles hewn in silver, decorated with navy and gray. They looked like fleas against the warmth and opulence of the meeting chamber. Nymm scanned each new arrival for the description of their target; the only detail they'd been given was that they would be wearing a purple cloak. But so far, the room was awash in a sea of grays and blues.

Finally, the Emissary emerged, preceded by a large contingent of the royal guard. Harp music accompanied her procession through the room toward the waiting officials, all of whom had stood—though some more graciously than others. Her long copper hair was woven into intricate swirls around her head, cascading down her back and over a shining golden dress. She looked like a live flame as she took her place at the last empty chair in the circle.

Nymm was startled by the fervor of the anger that coursed through her. She wished the Emissary had been the target, just so she could look her in the eyes. How could any of them sit here, eating cakes and making small talk, when her own home lay under rubble and ashes? Her own people, a fraction of the number they had been. Her own family tree would end with her, and none of them even cared.

Nymm focused her magic into the obsidian as the Emissary greeted her guests.

"I appreciate you all joining me here today. I hope you've been enjoying the festivities."

"Yes, yes." A tall, silver-haired man waved his hand through the air. "We know what your purpose was for calling the meeting on this day."

"The festival is … quaint," came from a serene woman to

the Emissary's left. "We could certainly permit you to continue to hold it, with some modifications."

Nymm struggled to hear each word. The Valmaran representatives' words were brusque, clipped. Their accents and staccato cadences did no justice to the lyricism of the Avernan language they barked out.

The Emissary's tone was incredulous. "The purpose of the festival is to honor the gods."

"You can still have your party. Perhaps we can incorporate prayer to the Conqueror instead."

"You're asking us to forsake our culture."

"It's outdated heresy," another man snapped. "And I don't know why any of you are entertaining the idea of letting it continue."

The Emissary leaned forward. "The terms of the treaty do not grant you influence over our religious practices. You overstep."

"The treaty," the same man replied in a mocking tone, "states that we may do whatever is necessary should we feel your actions threaten the sanctity of peace between our nations."

"Our worship threatens nothing!"

"It's barbaric! It's time you all became civilized. You're part of the continent now, and we won't have this spreading to our cities."

The Emissary stood. "I'd held this meeting in good faith, but I can see now that it was pointless."

A smaller man from across the circle stood. "Emissary, sit down. We've barely begun. Let's just—"

From behind the Emissary, out of the large, arched door strode a woman so small that she looked to be near Nymm's height. In her hands was a thick, worn tome bound in ink-black leather. Her coloring was unmistakably Civarran, her cloak a deep purple. Nymm was so shaken that she almost lost her handle on the magic recording their words. Why was she the target? Why was she even here?

"Who is this?" a woman closest to the door asked. All heads were turned toward the small woman who had strode into the center of their circle. She kept her gaze down to the floor, unmoving, as if she were one of the marble statues that decorated the halls.

The Emissary's voice boomed as she addressed the entire reception chamber. "Averna has been victim to Valmaris's will for too long. You push and you push, yet in your arrogance, you thought that we'd never push back. Magic is in our blood, though you tried to take it from us. Our people remember Civara, and our people love our gods. You've asked too much, and now we will not be asking."

As the Emissary finished her last sentence, the woman in the middle of the circle looked straight up at the ceiling toward the skylight Nymm was hovering over. Nymm shot back, chest heaving. Had she been spotted?

By the time she eased back into view, several of the dignitaries had risen from their chairs and were pounding at the doors lining the room. None of them would open. Some of their guards tried shouldering the thick wooden frames open themselves, while others advanced on the Emissary and the strange woman—who was now smiling up at Nymm.

She looked back down and opened the book she'd been clutching. The words she intoned were low, the vowels strange to Nymm's ears. It sounded like Civarran, but spoken backwards and disjointed.

Then, her hands started to glow a pale yellow, until the room was bathed in their light. She turned her head to the Emissary, who nodded and moved to stand behind her, a motherly hand on her shoulder. The woman cast her hand out in an arc, and what followed, Nymm could only describe as terror. Immediately, people started falling to the floor, clutching their heads in their hands as their screams pitched higher and higher. Black-tinged blood pooled from their eyes, ears, and wailing mouths.

The people left standing behind the woman watched with the dawning horror that they were next. She'd simply have to turn around, and they'd be killed in a matter of seconds. A few of the braver souls charged for where the women stood, and as if choreographed, the Emissary's stoic guards cut them down before they could cross even half of the room. Heads rolled onto the decorated floor, their blood glistening in the nearby candlelight and sun rays that beamed in from where Nymm watched on.

The woman turned and swiped her arm out once more, but it was messier, less precise. The beam of light that burst from her was too bright for Nymm to look at, and she shielded her eyes until it faded while chaos was unleashed below. The room was more glass than wood or marble, and all the windows shattered as one. It was a miracle the roof remained intact. The glass raining down almost sounded like the keys of a piano. But now, no one was screaming. There was no one left to scream.

The Emissary flinched back from the woman as she grew brighter and brighter. "That's enough!"

Nymm couldn't even see her, only hear her panicked voice: "I'm trying! I've lost control of the spell!"

Spell? It was a spellbook? Nymm had never heard of magic needing a spell. It simply ... was. Magic flowed from mages like breath or laughter, or tears. Anything crafted like a spell seemed far too powerful.

The Emissary unsheathed the sword at her waist, a decorative and heavy thing, and moved to strike down the mage. She first tried for her hand, and it fell to the floor, still casting that awful, brilliant light. The mage's screams filtered out of all the broken windows as she fell to her knees, clutching at her arm to slow the blood flow.

But magic wasn't a tool, an accessory. It was a living thing, as alive as the mage who wielded it. The Emissary realized this, realized what she must do. But it was of no consequence, because she was already too late.

All Ablaze

CHAPTER TEN

AUREN

Up on the rooftops, the sun beat down on Auren much more mercilessly than he'd imagined. He'd dressed in all white, so different from his usual dark ensemble. But with the sun still high in the sky, he would have been spotted immediately. Luckily, he'd been spared the ridiculous cloaks and masks the rest of them had donned when they'd set out that morning. But at the crown of his head, the tops of his shoulders, even his upper lip, he was drenched in a thin layer of sweat that made him want to go home and bathe. It didn't help that thus far, he'd seen nothing of note other than the occasional couple that took to the shadows, thinking they were much more discreet than they were.

He'd crossed a few rooftops to check in on everyone's stations. Ivan and Milo he'd seen recently. New and eager to please, they looked almost too alert for the casual partygoers they were passing for. Virgil waited in an alleyway too dense and obscured for Auren to keep tabs on him, so he'd have to trust that nothing had gone wrong.

Allara, he only caught glimpses of; her deep red cloak

blended in too well with the density and variety of the crowd. He'd enjoyed the musicians and magic displays he'd seen so far. His current fixation was on the grouping of guards on the adjacent rooftop, playing some sort of dice game and gambling trinkets from one of the stalls in the main square. They weren't all supposed to be there—Auren knew each of their routes by heart—but it was entertaining, and for the time being, it worked in his favor.

Auren crossed back to the rooftop that bordered the main stage in the square. He'd never much cared for the festival. The honoring-of-the-gods part was meaningless to him. Why pray for things to be in your favor when you could buy them? But this one, this time, brought a smile to his face. How could it not, when he'd be one of the richest men in Oberon afterwards, a living legend among the guilds?

Before his daydreams could take him further, his attention was drawn to the highest point of the Hold, where a beam of light shot up from the roof and straight up into the sky. What kind of show was that? He'd been to enough festivals to know the acts were kept to the stages; sometimes a fool or busker would take up at an alleyway with a pan out for gold, but nothing so grandiose as this. He supposed with the visiting dignitaries, the Emissary had requested that they put on a display.

Well, a display it was—until what Auren thought were shrieks of delight or awe morphed into screams of terror. The light from the tower faded, but something else had taken its place. Dark, moving masses began pouring from where the light had shone. At first, it looked as though the Hold had released all of their messenger ravens into the sky at once, but the masses were too frenzied and disorganized. Whatever they were, they started to get closer, a large contingent of them streaking through the sky toward the main festival courtyard.

Auren swore to himself and glanced around, not finding any of the Fools at their posts. But he couldn't stay where he was supposed to be stationed either. Across the way, the guards that had been gambling were now readied, spears and swords aimed toward the dark entities. All their armor and steel did them little good as dark blurs tore through the air at incomprehensible speeds. The closest guard went crashing down into the crowd below, his own sword impaling him as he met with the cold, hard ground. Another was knocked off his feet, but remained on the rooftop, a dark mass leaning over him.

Unmoving, Auren had a chance to get a better look at it. But he could've had all the time in the world to study it, and it wouldn't have been any more comprehensible. It was semi-transparent and writhing as if it were made up of pure smoke, and there were no discernible human features. But it didn't need hands to hold the guard down, or a mouth to feast on his flesh. His screams mingled with those of the crowd below, a twirling mist of inky black rising up from where he lay trapped under the creature.

Despite its lack of a face, Auren could tell when its attention shifted to him. Drawn out of the horrific trance he'd been in, he bolted for the edge of the rooftop and jumped to a neighboring building. This one had a worn, rickety ladder propped along the side, and Auren wasted no time sliding down it, forgoing the rungs entirely. His hands burned from the friction, but his feet hit the ground running, and he tore through the busy streets.

His instincts screamed at him to run away from these things, not toward them, but he fought the flow of the panicked crowd as he sprinted for the gates of the Keep. Nymm had been somewhere in there; if things were on schedule, she'd be in the exact tower he'd seen this all erupt from. She might need help getting out, and he couldn't rely on any of the Fools still being alive. He couldn't rely on her still being alive either, but he'd never be able to live with himself if he didn't do everything in his power to help her.

A small voice nagged at the back of his mind to turn around and run straight to Cyrie and his mother before it was too late. But they would be at home. Cyrie was always good for her word, and they were safer there. Nymm had no one else but him, and he wouldn't let her down.

As he ran through the streets, he dodged fallen citizens, some prey to these things, and some prey to the crush of the crowd. Windows shattered on both sides of the street, glass raining down on passersby as guards and citizens wrestled in vain against the unknown. He didn't recognize anyone he passed, but in the confusion, who was to say they weren't neighbors or friends?

If Auren didn't know any better, he'd say that demons had been set upon them. He'd never believed in the gods—not truly—nor the Above they supposedly inhabited. But were these creatures from the Below? And if they were, where were the gods now?

The screams got quieter as Auren approached the gates to the Keep. They were flung open and partially dented, as if someone had rammed them open just to escape. Most everyone who was left here was dead. Some lay in the street with eyes unseeing toward the summer sky, and with some, there were only traces of who they might have been—a shoe, a mask, a dark outline as if only their shadow remained, trapped by the sun. Auren's heart was beating so hard it was starting to feel like it wasn't beating at all.

There was no one to stop him or ask to see his credentials. The door wasn't even closed. Inside, guards and servants alike were dead. Pretty silver trays meant to collect drinks were scattered on the floor. Plant pots had been knocked over, leaves and soil spilling onto the warm marble.

Auren had studied the blueprints of the Hold, of course, but between the panic and the shock, he had trouble even remembering left from right.

Auren only hoped Nymm hadn't still been on the top of the tower when that beam of light went up.

He leapt over broken decorations and fallen bodies as he raced to the top level of the Hold. The carnage and destruction everywhere—it was the worst thing he'd ever seen. The smell was indescribable, like the tang of copper, the smoke from a pipe, and the sulfur of the worst sewer. It was so bad that he drew up the cloth that was tied around his neck, hoping to mask the stench enough to keep from retching.

Once he'd reached the fifth floor, adrenaline fueled him so relentlessly that it felt as if he'd barely climbed a few stairs rather than the endless spiral he'd just escaped from. He bolted straight down the hallway and past the circular atrium, into a receiving room that connected to the meeting chamber. Plush benches were strewn and splintered all over the small room, and art pieces hung in ornate gold frames were trampled across the floor. There were no bodies, no blood, and none of that awful smell.

Auren steeled himself. The door to the meeting chamber had been barred with a silver sword that he removed and brandished as he crept into the room. His mind was swirling with questions—how everyone had died, why they'd been locked in. From all the intel they received, it was supposed to be a formal meeting, not some sort of ambush.

All of the windows had shattered, leaving sparkling pieces of glass that picked up the sun's rays like confetti. He glanced back at the door he'd come through, finding it covered in the same sooty residue as the guards that had been attacked. Across the room was the same stain, as well as a few bodies slumped against the dark wood. Spears protruded from their abdomens, and their eyes tracked him lifelessly. Heads lay far from the bodies they belonged to.

The only bodies and bits of cloth that remained didn't look like Nymm's, but he could tell there had been so many more casualties left without a trace. He fought past the nausea swirling heavy in his gut, hoping he wasn't unknowingly walking past her remains.

From a dark shape at the center of the room, so still he'd thought it to be furniture, he heard a small whimper.

A cloaked figure lay in a fetal position right at the center of the ornate sunburst mosaic in the marbled floor. Behind lay a woman so ornately dressed that Auren could only assume her to be the Emissary. The irony to see her here like this… In all her finery, she looked to be made from the gold coins she was stamped on, as lifeless as a piece of metal. But the other figure still clung to their world, not yet ready to be taken to the Above.

Auren approached, but each step felt like lead. He caught a glimpse of black hair and dark skin. They twitched, but their body moved all wrong, choppy and harsh. His breaths came quicker, his vision whiting out at the edges. At last, despite every muscle in his body screaming for him not to move any closer, he knelt down next to the figure.

Their breath came out in sharp, short wheezes, and Auren was hesitant to move them at all. But he had to know. Slowly, he eased them onto their back, and saw a face far too young, far too similar to Nymm's. She was Civarran, although it wouldn't have been as readily apparent if he hadn't seen the hair under her cloak or the skin on her wrist—a singular wrist, because one of her hands sat separated from her, still open as if it were in the middle of grasping something.

She looked as though she'd been left in the sun for days, blistered and peeling. Auren reared back, withdrawing his hand as if it were something he could catch. Maybe it was. It was clear that whatever god or gods there may have been, Oberon was left to its fate. No true god would stand for this.

His hand tangled in her cloak in his haste to put some distance between them—her *purple* cloak. Shit. She was the target. He cursed as the whole job slipped through his fingers. Whatever had happened here, she was in no shape to be moved. There was no way to complete their end of the bargain.

Heart leaden, Auren made to stand, but the girl drew in a few rapid breaths, her eyes slowly cracking open. They were the same deep ocher as Nymm's. Had this girl suffered the same, or did she still have a family somewhere, waiting for her to come home? She looked as if she wanted to speak, but she was so weak that her breath wouldn't have even doused a single candle. Against his revulsion, Auren leaned in.

Her breathy words were so thin, like there wasn't enough air to carry them. "I'm sorry," was all she managed.

Auren leaned away. "What? Sorry for what?" He took in the room again, the carnage that it had endured. He looked at the ceiling directly above them and found a black burn ring, like the kind you'd make with light and a magnifying glass. Then his gaze fell to the upturned palm of her severed hand. Peeled-away, raw and angry skin. And then it all clicked.

"You did this?" His voice was barely above a whisper.

A single tear rolled from her eye in a burning path down her cheek. She didn't even possess the strength to blink it away. She met his eyes and looked as though she wanted to say more. But Auren didn't know if he wanted to hear it. How was she capable of this? What monsters had she unleashed upon the city? He needed to find Nymm, but he couldn't leave her to die alone. Whatever she'd done, whatever she had brought upon them, she didn't deserve to die alone on the floor. She looked as young as Cyrie, and he blinked away the terrible vision of her lying there instead.

Auren scooted closer to her, not wanting to touch her and cause her any pain, but for her to know that he was still here. Her breaths clawed their way from her lungs, and she made a primal, desperate sound. He glanced at her sleeve, lined with amethyst and some type of agate. This was magic, then. Of course something this terrible was not of the natural world. But he'd thought all the mages were gone—dead or in servitude. He'd never known them to be capable of *this*.

What he didn't understand was why—why she'd been set up for this, what was supposed to have happened. He agreed that most of the people in charge of Oberon, and of course Valmaris, could use some kind of retribution. But the average citizens, now being ravaged outside? This hadn't been for them. Ego drove actions like this, and everyone else paid the price.

Auren thought to rifle through his pouch and see if there was something for her suffering. Tulvar had explained all of the potions and poultices so well, but how could they have prepared something for this? Still, he uncorked a sleeping draught that at least might ease some of her pain. Her eyes widened so he could see the bloodshot whites. Had he scared her?

He shushed gently. "This might help. I mean you no harm."

But she wasn't looking at him. She was looking behind him, where a black, unnatural mass approached as if from thin air.

He didn't feel, he couldn't think. It was all over too fast.

CHAPTER ELEVEN
ALLARA

The Web was the last place Allara wanted to be, having spent so many nights there over the years that it held an unwelcome nostalgia for her. But just like she'd expected, everything had gone to shit, and she was going to get Taran out if it was the only useful thing she ever did.

As she neared the entrance, she stalled, pressed against a wall, chest heaving. Her whole body felt wrong, but with the amount of adrenaline coursing through her, that wasn't surprising. She'd marched all the way to the edge of the Middle Circle to the Web's closest entrance without a thought on how to get in. She didn't have a uniform, hadn't studied the blueprints or routes like Taran had. She steeled herself with a deep breath and headed to the front of the small cylindrical building, ready to weave a lie on her tongue.

But she'd worried for nothing. There was no guard at the front, and when she tried the door, there was no one in the holding room either. A few chairs sat to the left, and an empty, unmanned desk occupied the right. She headed straight ahead, to the door that led down to the underground. That too was unlocked and unguarded. For the many times Allara had been escorted in and out of this building, never had she seen it empty. It shouldn't have been empty. Unease filled her gut as she started down the steep, damp stairs. Lines and lines of cells stretched ahead of her once she reached the bottom. No windows, no light—it was impossible to tell how deep underground the Web actually was.

It was dizzying, the sheer number of cells in this stretch alone. Allara expected to be rushed by guards, jeered at by prisoners, maybe even to see a familiar face. But here, it was empty too. She picked up her pace, knowing now that something was truly wrong. It wasn't just The Fools; something terrible was happening during the festival. And she might be the only person paying any attention to it.

She raced down one hall, then the next, on and on. When the path diverged, she went right each time. If anything, she'd start back at the beginning and try the other way. Without her having any real idea of the danger they were all in, the only thing she was certain of was that time was against her. Every cell was as empty as the last, each guard post and office eerily vacated. If there'd been some kind of attack, then where were the bodies? The prisoners?

Allara was starting to get dizzy, frustrated. Her palms itched with sweat. Every hall looked the same, and she had no way to tell the time. She didn't trust any of her senses anymore. Finally, she took another right and almost ran into three guards, and she had never been happier in her entire life to run into one.

"Oh, thank the gods!" she began, out of breath. But her next words dried on her tongue when she met those familiar amber eyes. Taran was still in disguise. One of the guards with him had tawny skin and the strangest scab under his left eye, in the shape of an X. She didn't recognize either of them to be Fools, and Taran certainly seemed to be keeping up the act. She didn't want to out him; even though the job was ruined, they still needed to get away without getting arrested.

"There's a fight in the main courtyard. The festival. I came to get help." She hoped her breathlessness added to the lie, rather than making her look as suspicious as she felt. The other two men eyed her—the mask she'd let fall to her neck, the blood-red cloak that hung haphazardly across her torso. But then they looked to Taran, who gave a brisk nod. And then, wordlessly, they just left.

A jolt from her sense zapped through her, stronger than she had ever felt—a confusing mass she couldn't decipher.

Allara's brows crinkled together. "Taran?"

He sighed, his tone exasperated. "What are you doing, Allara?"

"What was that about?"

Not acknowledging her question, he continued, "What are you doing down here?"

"The job is compromised. We need to go."

He tilted his head slightly. "Compromised how?"

"I don't know." Allara let out a quick breath of frustration. "But someone got to Virgil. And Ivan. We can't wait around for them to get to us."

Taran stepped forward, laying a hand on her arm. "Calm down." He squeezed gently. "Take a breath."

Allara tried, closing her eyes, but there was a prickling at the back of her mind that snapped them open again. "Why did they just do what you said?" He hadn't seemed surprised that the job had gone bad, only that she'd come to find him.

"I don't know what you're talking about."

She tried to wrench out of his grasp, but his hold was firmer than she expected. She looked down at his hand, the yarn bracelet still hanging from his wrist—the only thing that remained of his oldest brother. "Taran, what's going on? What are you keeping from me?"

"Everything is fine, Allara. But you need to leave."

"Leave?" She met his eyes. "I came here to find you."

"You need to go, or you'll ruin everything."

"It's already ruined! We can't stay down here bickering and wasting time," Allara snapped, but Taran's grip on her arm only tightened. He drew closer to her, and she took a step back. Her skin felt hot where his fingers wrapped around it.

His frown was so small she almost missed it. "You weren't supposed to be here."

She sighed, frustrated. "I know, but you're not listening to me. The job—"

"Forget the job, Allara."

"How can you say that? You're the one who pushed me into this!"

"I had to."

"Why? We could have figured out another way, found another job."

"This isn't about gold. This is more than that." He let go of her and began pacing. "I wanted to tell you. I thought there would be a better moment than this. But you're so single-minded. You never see the big picture."

"What big picture?"

"We have the chance, right now, to make life better for all of Averna. But if I had told you, what would you have said? You're only concerned with your own needs."

"Daia is—"

"I know what Daia is," he snapped. "How many people like her do you think there are in Oberon? Across Averna? Who's looking out for them?"

Allara scoffed. "Do you mean yourself? Like you're some hero?"

"I will be, after today."

"You're not making any sense! What are you saying?"

"After my fight—the one I fixed? A Fool, Téo, did come to see me, but he wasn't the only one. After Téo offered me a job, I was offered the opportunity to join something—something bigger than either of us."

"And you accepted?"

Taran nodded.

"Then why take the job? Why drag me into this?"

Taran paused, and she knew she wouldn't like what he had to say next. "They needed me to get information back to them about what The Fools were doing. And I needed you to get the job."

"You *used* me? Used them?"

"It's not what I wanted, but it had to be done. I wish it could have been cleaner."

"You can't mean..."

"They would have spared you, Allara. I made sure of it." At the look in her eyes, he shook his head. "How could you even doubt that I'd protect you?"

"Nymm? Auren?"

"It's too late for them." He read her expression, brow creasing. "They were criminals! The world is better off without them."

"They're people! How can you be so callous?!"

"They were lying to the both of us. They knew what I knew, who the target is." His mouth turned down in a cruel smile. "Did you know there are still mages alive? Powerful ones?"

"The mages are dead. And what has that got to do with anything?"

"They'd hand over the last true mage for a bag of gold. A powerful mage! Someone who could fight for us, and they were going to just give her away."

"How do you know all this?" Allara thought back to her test, how he already knew The Fools. "Was Auren in on this too?"

Taran's laugh was bitter. "Gods, no. He's as mindless as the rest of them. But Virgil was more cunning than he let on. More self-serving too."

"So, he what? Sold them out?" Allara drew in a breath. "And he was killed for it."

"It's a small price to pay for a better world."

Allara's brows creased together. "How could you create a better world than this? Even the gods can't answer all of our prayers. You're just a man."

"I may be, but there are more of us than there are of the Valmarans. We've already gotten the prisoners out—enough for an army. Once Nymm grabs the mage, then we'll have her power at our disposal." His voice took on a frenzied pitch. "And once we get to the rest of the cities, more will join. They can't keep all of us down."

"So, you're part of some revolution now? And you think I'll just drop everything for this fantasy?" Allara's eyes filled with tears. "Taran, I'm all Daia has. How could you lie to me?"

"I know. And I'm sorry for that." He let out a breath akin to a growl. "You weren't supposed to come down here. Everything would have been taken care of."

Allara's heart dropped. "And now what?"

"I have to finish what I started. This will be good for us, Allara, you'll see."

Allara glanced around, not sure if she should run back the way she came or continue blindly through the maze. "Just stop for a minute. Listen to yourself."

"Will you come with me?"

"What?!" Allara held back a scoff. "No. And you don't need to do this either."

"Yes, I do!" he shouted, causing her to shrink back farther toward the bars. His eyes softened, but they were still so cold. This wasn't the person she'd grown up with.

"This is insane. I don't even know who you are right now."

"This is the most myself I've ever been. You just can't stand that I've done it without you."

Allara shook her head, looking down. "No, people are going to get hurt. People are already hurt."

"Only the ones who deserve it."

Allara had heard enough. She willed the tears not to fall, but they came anyway—for the boy she had loved, the man he no longer was. If she'd had more time to think on it, she'd realize all the moments he'd slipped away. The less she saw of him, the recklessness that would take him over... The anger he kept from bubbling up to the surface... It was all on display now. She took another step to the left, reaching down to her hip for her dagger.

Taran was too quick. Years of boxing, manual labor—and the gods knew what else. He grabbed both of her wrists. "This is your last chance, Allara. Be on the right side of history."

"I may agree with your cause, but your actions aren't right. You know it."

A moment of hesitation flashed across Taran's face, but he blinked it away. "My actions won't be remembered. Only the result. When the next generation is free from Valmaris's grasp, they'll remember us as heroes."

"Heroes don't do this." She leaned back toward him. "Please, just come with me."

The hand around her wrists tightened, then let go, and she breathed a sigh of relief. But instead of giving in, he pushed her into the nearest cell, slamming the door shut. "You have some time to think about all this. I know it's a lot, but you'll change your mind." He took a ring of keys from his belt, sliding them into the door. The click of the lock broke the last tattered piece of her heart.

"Taran," she choked out on a sob, "please, don't leave me down here!"

"I'll come back for you," he promised, as he backed toward where the other guards had gone.

"Taran!" she shouted after him, banging on the bars. He met her eyes one last time, then escaped around the corner without even a goodbye. Allara melted against the bars, letting her knees crash to the dirt. How could she be so stupid? Her best friend—her only friend—a rebel? A killer? How much of their relationship had been an act?

She cried even harder for Daia. Sweet Daia, with a voice like a fairy and a horrendous sense of humor. She was so weak now, and she wouldn't last long on her own. She'd need another dose of medicine in two days. Would Taran come back for her by then?

A sinking feeling in her gut had her wondering if he would ever come back at all.

Taran was like family to her. She thought they'd understood each other, that they both wanted the same things. A bond over fifteen years, ended with the click of a lock.

She'd known this job was trouble. If only she'd listened to her instincts two weeks ago and told Taran where he could stick his godsdamned job. Now she was stuck in the Web, entirely alone. No idea whether Nymm and Auren were even alive, and if they were, they had no clue where to find her. They'd probably assume she had abandoned them, wouldn't even try to look for her.

Allara's sobs were so forceful, she was worried she'd be sick. She thought to scream, bang on the bars—something. But she'd been through enough of the Web to know that it was empty. She looked around for something to dig at the ground with, but there was just a cot bolted to the floor and a useless wooden latrine. She fought back the shiver that crept up with the memories of nights she'd spent in cells identical to the one she now found herself in. She tried making leeway with her hands, but the ground was too hard-packed; all she did was splinter her already weak nails. She sat back, the cold seeping through her borrowed clothing.

She didn't even look like herself. She tore away her gilded mask, gaudy and ridiculous. What would Daia say when they found her here, dressed like this? She'd tease her for it. But Daia would probably be dead by then. And Allara would be too, or might as well be. Utterly alone. She'd been played for a fool twice over, and would have nothing but her regrets to keep her company.

There was no point in keeping the tears at bay any longer. The pain was too much. But something else swirled in her gut—something so horrific. It overwhelmed her sense, made her dizzy. She shot a hand forward to steady herself—and sparks emanated from it. She gasped, drawing her hand back, only to find it unharmed. It was as if she felt each vein, pulsing with the current of something new—something that had been dormant deep in her cells.

Her ears rang with distant screams she shouldn't have been able to hear. She clapped her hands over them, trying to drown out the sound. She couldn't explain it, had no idea what she'd peeked in on. But she knew, with an uncanny certainty, that even if she were to escape the Web, there was something much worse up above.

CHAPTER TWELVE
NYMM

When Nymm came to, she thought she'd lost both her sight and her hearing. Static drowned out everything else, and as she drew her hand from her ear, she found a thin trickle of blood, already drying. She thought she was seeing spots, black flecks that swam in her vision. But no matter the number of times that she blinked, they were still there, swarming, diving, slicing through the air like birds of prey. But there was something immediately unnatural about them, something that raised bumps on her skin and had her crossing her fingers over her heart. But she wasn't sure even her saints could protect her from this.

Miraculously, she was still up on the roof of the meeting chamber, bent over the beam of wood that had run between the panes of glass. She didn't want to look down; what had happened all came back to her in one sick rush. But she needed the obsidian, and to secure the target, or else it was all for nothing. Whatever was in the sky had moved below to the revelers at the festival. She'd have to be quick and hope whatever had been unleashed did not come back for her. Slowly, she righted herself and wondered how long she'd been out for.

Immediately, she felt lighter on her feet, faster. Her blood hummed—no, sang. It was as if the mere embers of magic she'd been bestowed at birth were now a raging inferno inside of her. The magic she'd buried for years felt as though it wouldn't be pushed down any longer, and the ferocity of it scared Nymm.

Whatever had been unleashed within that spell had awoken something in her she'd never felt before.

Getting back inside was less graceful than getting up to the roof had been. The bench she'd used for leverage to jump up had been flung across the room, so she landed on her feet and rolled to try to lessen the impact, but her ankles and knees still smarted. The atrium and receiving room were in disarray, and she knew the rest of the Hold probably looked similar. Keeping her eyes on the floor, she entered into the meeting chamber, doing her best to ignore the foul smell that lingered despite the heavy rush of air coming through each broken window.

Bits of glass, a river of blood, a lifeless hand or foot. She tried to keep her mind focused, looking for the shiny black stone among the intricate pattern of the floor, but her mind kept drawing her back to her childhood, to home. Her breathing came so quick that it made her vision swim, and she took a moment, closing her eyes and re-centering herself. When she first came to Oberon, she'd had many of these "episodes," until Shae taught her about grounding. She counted her breaths, tapped her fingers together, and focused on the sensation.

But she wasn't just remembering the horrors that had happened in Civara; they were happening here too. So, with each heavy step, she scanned the floor for the crystal and tried her best not to let her mind wander. She'd find it, make sure it was still intact, check on the target, and decide what to do next. She needed to gather The Fools somehow, see what was still salvageable from the job. But that would come after they were all safe from whatever was out there.

She was so high up, but the sounds from below seemed as if they were right outside the windows. It was utter chaos. Screams and fights, crowds running to get away. She and Auren would know to meet in the safe room below their warehouse, where Ilia and Tulvar surely already waited. But Virgil wasn't usually one for the field, and the rest of them were so new. She couldn't remember if they'd mentioned it in the briefing or not—what to do if it all went to shit … which it had.

She didn't come across the crystal in her perimeter search, so she started going across the room in precise rows. She tried not to linger on the bodies of the dignitaries and guards—those that remained, anyway. But a wrongness settled in her gut as she neared the center of the room. A ring of black surrounded the sunburst on the floor, but it looked to be ash rather than marble. She saw boots, so impossibly small, and the tattered remains of pants and the purple cloak that belonged to the mage.

But as her eyes continued to scan the floor, she saw another body. Older. Male. Dressed in threadbare white layers, torn and singed like they'd been dragged through a fire. Nymm's heart was in her throat. The clothes might not have sparked recognition, but it was the tanned hand outstretched toward the direction she'd come from that did. Dry, like it'd been drained of all blood. The malachite set in a brass band, looking as if it were a family heirloom.

Nymm fell to her knees, the sob tearing from her throat

matching the fervor from outside. She didn't want to look at his face—couldn't. She had enough corpses piled in her memory; she wanted to remember just one person alive, happy. He shouldn't have been here; he should have been far away, below ground by now. Nymm's heart cracked in two. He'd come to find her, save her.

Auren didn't deserve this.

It was the last straw.

Valmaris, Averna—the saints, the gods. They'd all gone too far, taken too much. Auren was the last person in the world she had left, her only family. And he'd died for her. Nymm sank farther onto the floor, eyes shrouded in a blanket of tears. The obsidian didn't matter anymore. The job didn't matter anymore. All Nymm had inside was a swirling mass of rage and sorrow. From now on, that was all she would be … if she even escaped whatever was outside, what had done this to Auren. Briefly, Nymm wondered why it mattered at all. Maybe she should just wait with him until she met the same fate.

Gaze averted, she reached for his face, running a hand along the side of it and closing his eyes. He'd never believed in the gods, the saints—nothing but gold. And her. He wouldn't want a prayer. So, she sat for a moment, quiet except for the sobs she tried to tamp down, and thought about him. His humor, the way he was quietly selfless, the way he brought life to everything he did. She tried to honor his memory, because that was the only thing left. His sister and mother hadn't deserved him; they never had. They hadn't seen the good in him like she had.

It took everything to draw herself away and stand, still keeping her eyes turned away. From the sound of things outside, she shouldn't linger. It was an awful place to leave him, among such a gross display of wealth. He deserved to rest under a tree in the countryside somewhere. Mancia or Asheron, maybe. Somewhere green, without the stink of sewers and corruption.

She knew he'd been trying to tell her he wanted to leave. But she had naively thought if she didn't let him say it out loud, that he'd change his mind, that she'd have time to convince him. And now he'd be stuck here for eternity. And she didn't have the strength to take him with her. So, instead, she pried the ring from his hand and secured it in her satchel. She didn't need its magic, but she needed some tangible way to remember him.

With heavy steps, she fled the chamber and began her descent down the winding stairs to get out of the Hold. Such a cursed, tragic place. She never wanted to see it again. She left the building, passing body after body, and the streets outside hadn't fared any better. Left and right, people were fleeing or fighting, trying to escape what Nymm could only describe as demons. A storefront to the right had caught on fire in the chaos, the thick, purplish smoke choking the sky above it. It would only be a matter of minutes before the surrounding buildings caught too, and what then? If it spread to the Outer Circle, so cramped and old, it'd make the perfect kindling.

Nymm ran and ran, taking advantage of any alleyway or shortcut she knew to get to the warehouse. There might be some hope that Tulvar or Ilia was still waiting there as instructed, and that the others had retreated when the chaos broke out.

She didn't want to see their faces when she told them about Auren. If she didn't, she could almost trick herself into having imagined the whole thing. But the second the truth of it passed her lips, it would be unchangeable, forever the end.

She slammed through the door of the building to find it

untouched from the briefing they'd had that morning. Or was it yesterday? The sun, while lower in the sky, still dragged on as the horrors unfolded, blending each atrocity into one single day.

Nymm tore through the rest of the rooms, flipping open the trap door into the safe house and finding it too to be empty. Tulvar and Ilia should have been here; there should have been some sign of them. If they had fled, where would they have gone? To the docks, maybe? They could be halfway across the island by now, or on the ocean. Nymm leaned against the wall, catching her breath and trying to collect her thoughts.

She was the one who came up with the plans; she always had a way to get through everything. But not this time. She'd lost too much, and the odds were insurmountable.

The smell of smoke wafted through the uneven doorframe and cracked windows, signaling to Nymm that she was out of time. If any of the Fools were still alive, they'd probably have the sense to get out of the capital. She had no idea how she'd ever find them, but she knew she'd have to try. She wondered if Shae would make it out, would even know what was going on. They'd both be running again, fleeing a home from violence and destruction again. With a little luck—or help from the saints—they'd find their way back to each other. When they'd both lost so much, maybe they wouldn't have to lose each other too. It was a vain thought, that her betrayal could be forgiven. But Nymm had to hope for it, because there was nothing else left.

She raced through the crowded city streets, dodging fellow fleeing citizens, overturned carts full of belongings, and the bodies that were piling up in the streets. It looked as if war had ravaged Oberon—and maybe it had. Whatever purpose the Emissary had planned to use the mage for, to whatever end, it certainly wasn't for peace. It had all gone too far out of control.

The docks were just as bad as the city's streets, the whole wharf in disarray. Some ships were already tiny specks in the distance, while others had sailors and passengers clambering aboard with hastily packed bags. A fight broke out on the dock by the dinghy nearest Nymm. A man getting ready to push off fought with a father trying to get his family on board. The passengers behind him argued, some shouting that there was no room, and some pleading for compassion. But with one final push, the sailor untethered the boat, and the man fell back onto the rickety, wooden dock. Wasting no time, he ushered his family to the next boat in the line that appeared to have some room.

Shaking her head, Nymm decided a boat wouldn't be the best option. And where would she go? Valmaris would be a different kind of death sentence. The Republic Isles, maybe? But she couldn't stand the uncertainty, the feeling of being a refugee yet again. Oberon might be burning now, but it wouldn't be that way forever. She needed to stay in Averna and figure out how to come back from this. Find the Fools that were still alive, and—saints willing—make someone pay for Auren.

So, instead, she cut back through the city, winding around the Middle Circle and back into the Outer Circle to the stables. Here too was in an uproar, but at least this time it worked in her favor. She would need all the gold she still had on her person for wherever she ended up, so she crept through the half-empty stables toward a deep gray mare. She didn't have time to settle her in like the horse deserved. She hopped on bareback and eased her into a gallop, ignoring the way her stomach dropped as the shouts of the stable master followed her into the air.

She was alive, still free, and not without some skills. She

had her wits and her magic, and she had a lot of work to do. They'd all gotten away with far too much—the Inner Circle ignoring the pain of Oberon's people, Valmaris invading and destroying countless lives, even Averna bending to Valmaris's will. But it wouldn't be that way for much longer. Nymm counted on it.

CHAPTER THIRTEEN
TARAN

It was the longest day of the year, and it couldn't have been over soon enough. The eerie glow of the moon cast the city in a sickly bluish tinge as the boat got farther and farther away. The orange peaks of the flames reflected brilliantly against the waves as Taran watched his city succumb to fire—and something worse.

Something had been unleashed—not part of the plan, and not of this world. Instead of staying to secure the city, their contingent of rebels and newly freed prisoners had fled to the water so they could dock at Fiora and regroup. None of them were stupid enough to think they stood a chance against whatever evil stalked Oberon's streets. But the plan could still work—they could still do this. Taran repeated that to himself over and over, because after what he had seen, he wasn't so sure anymore.

Now, they didn't have just Valmaris to contend with, but maybe demons themselves. And what he had done...

He could only hope his family had smelled the smoke, or heard that something was amiss, and gotten out in time. Having their own boat meant their odds were better. But they'd only ever lived in Oberon, so he couldn't guess at where they would go, or how he'd find them again. His stubborn mother might rather be consumed by the flames than abandon what she'd spent her life working to build. She had raised seven children in that home. Lost one, saw another married. All the recipes she'd tested and saved to buy special ingredients for, painstakingly written into a bound book and illustrated by him... The notches scratched into the beams of the wall as each of them grew... He feared she would refuse to leave it.

And Allara. He truly had planned to come back for her, before he realized what was going on up above. He had hoped she'd come around; if things had gone to plan, she might have. But the cause was greater than either of them; it was about all of Averna. She had to understand that. She might even be safer locked below, underground, where those things didn't roam.

But the what ifs and maybes did little to ease the heaviness in his heart, the guilt. Oberon would have to survive. His loved ones would have to survive. He didn't know what he'd become if either of those things weren't true. And deep down, he knew there was a chance he would never see any of them again.

From their distance, the city looked like one of the festival lanterns, all ablaze. The others on their small rowboat seemed just as sober as him, shocked by what had become of this. They knew the risks of war, what could happen. But their first victory was also their first defeat.

The mage's magic must have been the cause of this. As they had been so close to the blast, he doubted that she or any of the dignitaries had survived. What glee he might have felt at having cut off so many of the serpents' heads paled at the loss of the mage. Their great bargaining chip, gone up in smoke. So much of their plan had hinged on securing her, utilizing her. Not only was she likely dead, she had left a wicked tear in the very fabric of their world.

The Emissary's death would also throw Oberon into even more chaos than they'd planned. They had to keep going. There were so many cities that still needed to be freed before all of Averna was independent again, before they weren't under Valmaris' boot any longer. Taran still couldn't quell the worry that they'd already lost what they had worked so hard to protect, that all of their other plans would turn to ash like this. But as he stared back at his city, he had to hope that what was lost in the flames would be rebuilt into something greater than they had ever imagined.

All across Averna, something was waking up. It clawed and fought itself onto this plane, with a ferociousness that would not be put back, sparkling and raw. Magic was back in Averna, and it would change everything.

The Tales of Averna will continue…

ACKNOWLEDGEMENTS

I started this book in June of 2020. I needed a distraction like so many of us did, and had always loved to write. But I had never written a full novel before, and after tinkering with the first three chapters for nearly a year, the manuscript sat forgotten on my computer.

Then, in 2023 I wrote *Golden Ruin*, and I realized that, yes, I am capable of writing a book—even if I have no idea where I'm going the whole time. So, once I published it I returned to that forgotten manuscript, with characters I was already fiercely protective of and a world I wanted to dive back into.

Though this is my second book and about half the size of *Golden Ruin*, it was undoubtedly harder to get the words onto the page. I struggled with the thought that yes, I had done this before, but could I do it again? But I did. And I love this book, this world, and I'm excited to bring you more in the next book of this series.

As I finished my final draft of this story, I wrote it in my grandma's kitchen on the digital typewriter I'd managed to grab as we'd evacuated from one of the several fires that broke out across Los Angeles at the start of 2025.

There I was, writing about a city that catches on fire for a book called *FIREREND*, when the horrors of that reality were ravaging neighborhoods like the Pacific Palisades, Malibu, Altadena, and more. *Should I even finish this book? Is it insensitive to let it see the light of day?* I was lucky enough to return home as I struggled with these thoughts.

You know the conclusion I came to as you're holding this

book in your hands. But to say it's just fiction, that it's just a story for fun, isn't enough. Real pain and tragedy are reflected in fiction, along with our hopes and dreams. So, I decided to tell the story I'd been itching to tell for the last five years, but I also can't pretend there isn't a real-world impact on some of the themes and events I've put into this book.

A portion of sales from *FIREREND* will be continually donated to the nonprofit, WatchDuty. Their app helped me and so many others to keep ourselves safe as fire after fire spread through our city. It is truly a testament to the good that can be achieved when we're looking out for each other.

FIREREND wouldn't have made it into your hands without the help of some incredible people.

Thank you to Emma, Louise, Max, and Riley, who sorted through the rubble of the first draft and helped me to find all of the gems.

Thank you to Kal and Robin for your expertise in editing this into the best story it could be.

Thank you to Charlie for creating another beautiful cover.

Thank you, dear reader, for taking a chance on this story. It is so dear to me and I hope that you felt a bit of the magic I've tried to create.

Lastly, thank you to my family. I am always grateful for your love and support, who I am and what I do is because of you.

More to come. <3 Emma.

ALSO BY EMMA KENNEDY

GOLDEN RUIN

Adult sapphic sci-fi/western

Follow Cassidy as she travels to one of the last two remaining towns in a dystopian California as she hunts for a cure to save her life. She might find more than she was bargaining for in this dangerous but charismatic town.

ABOUT THE AUTHOR

Emma Kennedy is a science fiction and fantasy author from Los Angeles, California. Her favorite stories are ones about people—their problems, their love, and their humanity. When she's not writing you can find her making candles, playing video games, or going on an adventure. Keep in touch online to follow along with the Tales of Averna series and everything else Emma is working on.

instagram.com/emmakennedywrites

threads.net/@emmakennedywrites

tiktok.com/@emmakennedywrites

pinterest.com/emmakennedywrites

goodreads.com/emmakennedywrites